I0552526

ZOJJED v2.0

THE END OF CIVILITY

By Jeff and Jennifer Salvage

First Edition

Copyright 2019, Salvage America Publications

978-1-7335757-3-7

ACKNOWLEDGEMENTS

There are many people to thank for the accuracy and professionalism of Zojjed v2.0.

Technical Advisers: William Regli, PhD., Marcus McCurdy, Sean Grimes, and John Perez, ESQ.

Editing and Storyline Input: Michael Hirsch, Ann Schwartz, Susan Lewis and Frank Lewis.

Cover Model: Robyn Stevens

DISCLAIMER

This book is a work of satirical fiction. The majority of the events and characters described here are imaginary and are not intended to refer to specific places or living persons. The exception is any quotes or tweets by President Trump. They are actual statements made by President Trump with the exception of the names of people in the statements being changed to match the characters in the book. Yes, truth is stranger than fiction.

Many facts and statistics have been referenced in our bibliography in the back of the book.

CHAPTER ONE

Alex Pinto's heart was pounding. While her Garmin indicated it was pulsing at 180 beats per minute, she had years of race walking experience and didn't need electronics to tell her she was pushing past her limits. Her gasping breath and dry, salt-encrusted skin told her she was close to crashing. Even though the race started at the crack of dawn, it was now past 8:00 AM and the mercury had climbed into the upper 80s. The heat of the Mexican sun combined with the saturating humidity should have made her sweat profusely, but when she made the turn on the utilitarian 2 km course, she felt her dehydration hit a critical level. Still, she pushed on, hearing her competitors closing in on her as her body betrayed her once again.

Alex could see the start/finish line in the distance. It wasn't a glamorous show like at the Olympics or the World Championships, but at the Pan Am Cup in Lázaro Cárdenas, Mexico, it was all that the budget afforded. No flashy lights, live video feed, or illuminated DQ board. Instead, a simple structure littered with the IAAF (International Amateur Athletics Federation) logo as well as the names of a few sponsors loomed ahead. For Alex, it couldn't be coming up fast enough.

"Drive your hips", "Keep your arms down and back", "Turnover, turnover, turnover!" she screamed internally to herself. She needed to raise the mantras she had drilled into her subconscious over a 20-year race walking career to her conscious mind late in the race. Alex felt her form improve giving her the illusion she was in control.

The large crowds that lined the street helped. Enthusiastic, local fans chanting "USA, USA, USA," gave an adrenaline rush that just didn't happen when racing in the States. The success of Mexican race walkers from the 70's and 80's grew a strong and passionate following for "La Caminata" as race walking was known south of the border. Amazingly the anti-immigration policies of the Trump administration didn't dampen their enthusiasm. Regardless of politics, Mexican fans were always supportive of walkers from their northern neighbor. This was true whether they were doing well in the race or painfully hobbling in the back of the pack.

Unfortunately, Alex knew her pace was slipping. Every race walker that approaches the competition has a different goal. Alex hoped to at least achieve her international PR by walking her fastest time in competition outside of the United States. Often, she would walk her best performances in trial races only to falter once she got to the bigger stage. Walking by herself, and well under her projected pace for the first half of the 20 km race, she was confident that she was going to crack the puzzle of peaking at the right time. But at this point the 10km mark seemed like a marathon ago.

Now as the start/finish line of the IAAF Pan American Cup race came into focus, she could see the seconds ticking by 1:28:01, :02, :03. She estimated in her head that she could cross in 1:29:30, but she was not racing alone. This was no time trial and like most walkers she had more than one goal in a given race. Sometimes, she set a goal for a time, a place, and to beat certain competitors simultaneously. Tempted as she was to see who was coming, she didn't look back. Long ago, she was scolded by her high school coach that the race was in front of her and not to concern herself with what was going on behind her.

As she got closer, she could hear the chants change to "Vamos, Vamos, Vamos" and "Si se puede." Clearly, with the Mexican squad approaching, they turned their attention to their favorites telling them to "Go! Go! Go!" and that "Yes, you can!" But, could Alex? She repeated her mantras, knowing she had to focus on the process of winning, not the winning itself. *"Focus only on each step, not what's going on around you,"* she could hear her coach echo in her head.

As his voice dissipated, so did her view of the start/finish line when in a blink, she was swallowed by the lead pack. The small cadre of six athletes were from a diverse set of countries. Mexico had two women in the mix, but so were walkers from Peru, Brazil and Ecuador. Surprisingly, one walker from the USA was hanging on to the back of the pack. Jennifer was a young phenom who was the first legitimate hope for USA race walking in a decade.

One of the great attractions of race walking is the diversity of people on the podium. Unlike the sprint events that are constantly dominated by a few countries like the USA and Jamaica, the race walk is a free-for-all. Race walking is a sport for everyone. A combination of few resources required to train, dearth of interest from the general public, and longer duration of the event led to a wide range of countries fielding competitive race walkers.

With just 200 meters to go, someone needed to break out, but break out carefully. Race walking is not a freestyle event. Much like the butterfly or backstroke in swimming, it requires conformity to a style of ambling. One foot must remain in contact with the ground (at least to the human eye) and the leg is required to be straightened from the moment of contact with the ground until it reaches the vertical position. These athletes know the rules well and conforming to them was second nature. However, pushing towards the finish in such a tight group was sure to create issues for those a hair less fit than the best. In the past many walkers had their medal snatched away by an ever present judge watching for infractions. While in general it takes four judges to disqualify a racer, in the last 100 meters, the chief judge can disqualify you with a single glance. The athletes had to remain hyper-vigilant.

The pack's sweat rained behind their bodies, soaking Alex who couldn't concern herself with the leaders. Alex's pace wasn't able to keep up and with the adrenaline rush gone, she started to fade. The reality for Alex wasn't good. She wasn't just a few steps behind the leaders when she crossed the start finish line, she actually had two complete laps to go. Like most US race walkers, she wasn't even close to the world's best. Alex, similar to many athletes, tricked herself into thinking she was racing with the lead pack to get an added push. But now the sobering truth was that 4km's of walking remained, sapping her legs, hips and arms of any strength.

Alex attempted to cheer Jennifer on, but all that came out was a faint chirp "Go." Alex wondered if it was even audible or if she just spoke it in her head. *"Focus Alex,"* she repeated to herself.

As the crowd appropriately fixated on her competitors' achievements, she pushed out for the lonely, late journey.

"Maybe you shouldn't have stayed out last night," barked a member of the Canadian team. Usually, US/Canadian camaraderie was tight, but Ilia was a former Russian athlete who emigrated to Canada after, like many Russian race walkers, he failed a drug test for doping. After serving a four-year suspension, he switched allegiances and aligned with Athletics Canada, the Canadian athletic federation. Some walkers felt he served his time and were okay with his return. However, Alex overheard a drunken boast from Ilia stating, "I'd rather dope than be slow." Alex was disgusted by Ilia as were the majority of the clean athletes. *"It's only race walking,"* thought Alex. *"How could you possibly want to win that badly?"*

Somehow Alex fired off a "Fuck off Dopey," with what was left of her strength. She wasn't sure if he knew the nickname he was given by the honest athletes, but figured he'd get the message. Alex tried to shake Ilia's antagonism, but deep down she knew he was right. She hadn't focused on the race last night, but now it was time to concentrate and knock off the last 4K without death marching. Alex had seen too many of her friends look great for 15K, only to stagger to the end like a walking corpse.

Fortunately, some relief was in sight. Misting showers were dead ahead as was the aid station that followed. She slowed her pace even more as she soaked herself under the showers. She could feel her body temperature lowering and grabbed both water and electrolyte gels as she passed the personal refreshment table where each athlete was allowed to stock the table with beverages and gels of their choice.

Usually, replenishing fluids was enough to give an athlete a temporary boost, but Alex had pushed too far and was at the point of no return. The slow petrification of her legs impeded her progress as more competitors passed her. *"You have to finish,"* she told herself. She could see Ilia mocking her at the after-race party if she didn't. Thoughts of her technique went out the window and forward progress was all she could think about. Then she received a rude awakening as a yellow paddle with a "<" symbol was flashed in front of her face by a judge. The symbol signified that she was in violation of the bent knee portion of the definition of race walking. Hell, at the pace she was walking she definitely didn't have both feet off the ground simultaneously, she was walking so slow judges could easily see both her feet were on the ground for an extended period of time.

"Shit! Focus. You can do this," Alex challenged to herself. In general, Alex had a very legal race walking style, but like all athletes, when drained of energy, her technique suffered. Her very untraditional injury from college also plagued her. She never quite got over the explosion at the stadium that killed her favorite college professor and left her foot a mangled mess. Years of therapy first got her walking again, and then eventually got her strong enough to race walk. However, she was never again considered an Olympic hopeful.

As she marched on, she focused solely on making sure her knee was straightened on impact and forced it to stay that way despite the cries of her cramping shin muscles. When shin muscles tighten, it's almost impossible to keep the knee straightened properly, but with only about 3km to go at this point Alex felt she could muscle through it. Just then the world started to darken and then go pitch black.

CHAPTER TWO

Agents Bob Traya and Mira Tano were crossing a finish line of their own. Government lifers, they were both hired shortly after graduating college. They joined the Department of Homeland Security when it formed in 2002, and have worked behind the scenes at a satellite office in Virginia ever since. Typically, they gathered and analyzed data, but today they were just sitting back and watching a live feed as another child trafficker was arrested. Jeffrey Epstein was the big name people associated with the unconscionable crime of human sex trafficking, but there were countless other perpetrators with even more victims.

Amazingly, before the year 2000, human trafficking wasn't even a federal crime. The relatively new law had limited effect in the US, which is one of the world's worst offenders. Some estimates of human trafficking were as high as hundreds of thousands of victims across the country and almost 20,000 new victims every year. With 150 new calls coming into the National Human Trafficking Hotline every day, they struggled to promptly address them all.

The breadcrumbs of human trafficking are all over the Internet. One just needs to know where to look for them. While you can't find anyone other than the perhaps an Amish grandparent who isn't familiar with how to Google something, Google isn't very effective at helping search for human traffickers. Google's algorithms are quite advanced and are great at predicting relevant content in most cases. It's so effective that many right-wingnuts accuse Google of being biased in their results. The dirty secret is they are biased, to science and mathematically-based truths. When someone Google's climate change, it's not going to show "studies" funded by oil companies to deny the obvious; instead it's going to present articles from sites like NASA and those that have been properly peer reviewed.

NASA: Climate Change and Global Warming

https://climate.nasa.gov

Vital Signs of the Planet: Global Climate Change and Global Warming. Current news and data streams about global warming and climate change from NASA.

Climate change: How do we know? - Evidence | Facts ...

https://climate.nasa.gov › evidence

Most of these climate changes are attributed to very small variations in Earth's orbit that change the amount of solar energy our planet receives. Scientific ...

IPCC — Intergovernmental Panel on Climate Change

https://www.ipcc.ch

The Intergovernmental Panel on Climate Change (IPCC) is the United Nations body for assessing the science related to climate change. Previous website ...

Google is optimized for selling. Which is fine in most cases, but that doesn't help law enforcement. Where Google really falls short is in its reach. While they've indexed over 130 trillion pages to date, they are just scratching the surface of the information available on the Internet. That's because the majority of the Internet is hidden from Google's prying eyes.

Unseen by Google are many forms of information that aren't easily understood by Google's indexing machines like multimedia content. Additionally, there are countless websites that are blocked by password protection called the deep web. These sites belong to law abiding companies that need to protect their intellectual property.

While the majority of this unseen material may be harmless, there is a seedier side to the Internet called the dark web. It's where illegal activities including selling of illicit substances, weapons, financial fraud and of course human trafficking occur with anonymity. One time a region explored only by Internet pioneers, it's now relatively easy to creep into the dark web by downloading a special browser called TOR and taking the proverbial plunge.

Agents Traya and Tano had a not so secret weapon. DARPA, the research wing of the military, sponsored an open source project, Memex. Memex is a collection of software tools developed under DARPA's lead, which allows law enforcement to better search the Internet for nefarious activity.

Before the creation of Memex, searching anything not indexed by Google was an incredibly manual process. Even when data was catalogued properly, correlating one finding to another was a laborious task.

Memex changed all of that with its powerful scraping engine designed to crawl within the Internet far beyond Google's capability. For starters, it doesn't just search the visible surface portion of the web, but can be directed to search deeper and into the darker corners of the Internet.

Where human traffickers could previously obfuscate themselves from search engines by hiding information in images, Memex could analyze photographs for content like a young girl holding up a phone number and extract the number. With the advances in computer vision, automated data can be gathered that included the age, sex and even the emotion of people in a photo or video.

Similarly, if the human trafficker used an email address, the same extraction could occur. By the nature of the business, there had to be a way to contact the trafficker to arrange the deal, so they had to advertise contact data one way or another. Memex allowed law enforcement to turn their advertising against themselves.

Memex took it further by creating tools to allow the aggregating of data and cross-referencing it with other information gathered from traditional ground intelligence to, over time, build a map illustrating the patterns of perpetrators.

With these tools at their disposal it was significantly harder to hide from law enforcement, as was evidenced on Traya and Tano's screen as they watched John Wartell being led out of his house in handcuffs.

CHAPTER THREE

Miguel could hear the owner screaming obscenities in Spanish not too far behind him. "Bastardo, estúpido!"

He would be armed of course, given the proliferation of guns in Mexico. While officially, there was only a single sanctioned gun shop anywhere in Mexico and the paper trail required for a legal gun is long and arduous, the black market for guns outnumbered legal purchases over ten to one. The source of the majority of the illegal weapons is just north of the border, the USA. This rise in gun access has led to an average of 10,000 gun related deaths a year in Mexico.[i]

Eyes darting and heart pounding, Miguel looked down the street to his left. Clutching the Guanabana fruits he just snatched from the open air market, he knew he needed to disappear. His mother loved this peculiar food, a combination of strawberry, citrus, and banana. He decided on a good exit plan and ran down the narrow alley. He jumped into the dumpster without hesitation and settled in until he could no longer hear the angry, hate-filled shouts of the vendor. Emerging from the refuse, Miguel hopped the fence and headed home.

"Mama," he called as he opened the screen door covered in duct tape to keep out the flies, "I'm home."

Miguel found his mother in the kitchen doing dishes. He proudly plunked the prized fruit down on the table. This was met with a stern frown, "Miguel, how many times do I tell you that it is a sin to steal?"

He averted his eyes and tried, "Mama it fell off the truck?"

She clucked and wagged her finger at him, "Go see your amigo Jefe, maybe he can talk some sense into you. He has good morals."

Miguel knew better than to argue with his mother and he headed off to see his best friend. Jefe was sitting out on the front step and smiled when he saw Miguel. They went into the empty lot across the street to kick a fútbol ball around. Jefe's mother waved from the kitchen and smiled. Jefe and Miguel fantasized about getting their families out of Mexico City and away from the danger which lurked around every corner. Jefe had been approached by MS-13 on more than one occasion but stood his ground and wouldn't be forced into being a *violent slave*. MS-13 wasn't as active in Mexico as many of the other ruthless gangs. *"Just my luck they would take over my neighborhood,"* Jefe thought on more than one occasion.

A car pulled up to Jefe's house sounding like it was in desperate need of a new muffler. They continued to pass the ball back and forth until they heard the sound of glass shattering and a piercing scream. The ball rolled to a stop as both Miguel and Jefe froze in fear. The screams were guttural and did not sound human. Mateo walked out of the house yelling, "I told you there would be payback for defiance!" In his right hand he held a large machete used to clear the jungle. In his left hand he clutched a fistful of blood-soaked hair still clinging to the head that swung listlessly back and forth.

Miguel let out a raucous scream. It was dark and he couldn't see, all he could feel was pain searing through his veins. Hearing the scream, his Aunt Rosa ran into his bedroom, "Miguel , it's okay. You're safe."

Miguel tried to catch his breath and squeezed his eyes shut. He could still see Jefe's mother's severed head. It was a memory he just couldn't shake whether he was awake or asleep.

"You had a nightmare, mi sobrino. You are here, you're not in Mexico. Those horrid men can't hurt you now."

Miguel blinked trying to wash the image away. "Julia?" he asked voice trembling.

His aunt took his hand, "You know her. She slept through it, didn't hear a thing."

CHAPTER FOUR

"Not again!" she grumbled. Alex awoke on a table in the med tent. As her head cleared, the reality of her failure came into focus.

Not being a member of the official USA team, there was no one assigned to look after Alex during or after the race. One reason she was competing at the Pan Am Cup was because they allowed guests. Often, she would travel to the larger championships and only be a spectator or volunteer. However, with the opportunity to toe the line with some of the world's best walkers, how could she not grab the chance?

Then, she felt a friendly hand grip hers. It was Caidy, one of the walkers from the USA team and fellow competitor that day.

"Don't try to get up Alex," Caidy stated in a calming voice.

"Ugh, I'll be fine," Alex attempted to reassure her. Then, she tried to change the topic. "How did you do?"

"Not as well as Jennifer. She rocked a third-place finish. But, I faired a little better than you. I snuck under the qualifying time for Doha," Caidy replied. Doha is the capital of Qatar and is where the next IAAF World Championships were being held. It was every elite race walker's goal to qualify for it.

"I was just here getting a post-race massage when they dragged you in and I came over to check on you."

"You are such a good friend Caidy," Alex trying to make light of her situation, she deflected stating, "take care of yourself, I'll be fine."

"Well Alex, at least I am not leaving the course with a souvenir," continued Caidy.

"Oh no, now what," thought Alex and she instinctively raised her hand to her head, only now realizing the bruise there was throbbing. As more of her reality came into focus, she also realized there was an IV sticking into her other arm, filling her full of badly needed fluids.

The bag was almost drained. *"Shit, how long have I been here?"* thought Alex.

Even though Caidy was a good friend and she outclassed Alex on the track, they still had a bit of competitive rivalry. Sometimes that spilled over and off the track in less than friendly ways. Caidy decided to tease a little and volunteered, "It's not your first bag."

"How long have I been out?" Alex inquired.

"Ha, just kidding. You've been in and out of it for a little bit. They've been checking on you regularly."

Just then, the unwanted eye of Munson Grayson popped into view. Munson, or Munse as the team like to call him, was the top 50km walker on the USA team. A true millennial, he vlogged everything. As if he had a sixth sense, he was always where the action was, and nothing was taboo. Clearly, the med tent was no exception.

"Munse, get the hell out of here," ordered Caidy with an authority that made him jump back, but with the camera rolling and a ridiculous smile on his face.

Simultaneously, the medic in the tent realized Munson's intrusion and ushered him away.

With Alex on the mend, Caidy settled on a nearby massage table while plugging her phone into a small public charging station T-Mobile set up for the athletes to use.

"Don't do that!" warned Alex.

"Do what?" asked Caidy.

"Use a public charger like that. They can be infected," Alex explained.

"With germs? don't worry I don't get sick."

"Silly, no with a computer/phone virus. It's the next wave of cyber-attack."

Caidy laughed, "Maybe you hit your head harder than you thought. You worry way too much. You see threats everywhere."

CHAPTER FIVE

For the second time that day Miguel felt his heart pounding so hard and fast he was sure a cardiac emergency was on the way. *"Maybe that would be best,"* he thought. Miguel was just an hour from his home while driving in South Jersey. He hoped he wouldn't lose everything he worked so hard protect from a random police check point. He looked longingly at the photo hanging from the rear view mirror on his rosary beads and said a prayer. His five-year-old daughter had his eyes and her mother's impish smile.

"Deep breath, Miguel focus!" There is no reason to panic, your paperwork will hold up to the cursory check. He rolled down the window and with slightly trembling hands presented his license and registration.

The police officer glanced at the papers. Then, he walked around to the back of car to check the license plate. He shook his head with tired disdain. *"Of course,"* the officer thought, the undocumented immigrants were always from Maryland since Maryland doesn't require proof of residency in order to get a driver's license. He didn't have the energy to deal with the mountain of paperwork that would follow if he detained him, so he handed the documents back and waved him on.

Miguel drove a few blocks and then pulled onto a side street to regain his composure. His phone chirped indicating that that there was an Uber client requesting a driver. He clicked "Accept" and found he was headed to the Philadelphia airport. Airport jobs were a great opportunity. People leaving town were always generous and relieved to get there on time. Then you could catch a client needing to go home and they were even more generous and happy to be home no matter where they were. He drove from Cherry Hill, NJ a few miles to Marlton to pick up the rider, Rachel. She was very pleasant but not the most talkative client which was fine because Miguel was still coming down from the adrenaline rush caused by the brush with the local authorities.

Almost immediately after dropping Rachel off at airport, a new job popped up. He accepted quickly and found the ride was headed from the airport into the city to the Center City Hilton Hotel. As the rider got in the car, he introduced himself as Leon, and asked about the photo hanging from the mirror.

"I'm Raul," Miguel replied. Miguel hated lying to his customers, but in order to get a job at Uber you had to pass a background check to make sure your driving record is relatively clean and you don't have a significant criminal record. While they don't require that you are a citizen and do not check explicitly for permit to work, they do require your social security number for the background check. Miguel's friend Raul left the United States, because his mother was very ill and needed him home to help with their affairs. He was kind enough to "lend" Miguel his number.

Miguel beamed and told him about his daughter Julia who was being looked after by his Aunt. After a few minutes, he stopped and apologized, "I am sorry to talk so much but when it comes to my daughter, I just can't help myself. Please tell me what brings you to Philadelphia."

"I am a surgeon from Montenegro," explained Leon.

"Montenegro, really. That's a first in my car!" exclaimed Miguel. He made a mental note, one more country to the list. A few of his Uber-driving friends had an informal competition for the who had driven people from the most countries. Adding Montenegro still put him ten behind.

"It's an amazing country. We are actually one of the newest countries, only declaring independence in 2006, but we have a rich history. We are home to the oldest olive trees in the world!" Leon said with pride.

"Muy Bien, what brings you so far from home?" asked Miguel.

"I'm here for a medical convention."

Miguel knew he had 20 minutes to Leon's destination and having influential friends in other countries is never a bad thing for a man in Miguel 's position.

"What is the convention you will be attending?" Miguel inquired to break the seal.

"Actually, I am one of the keynote speakers. I will be presenting my research on the post-traumatic stress in adults who were forced into performing violent acts as children. There were a lot of atrocities during the Yugoslov wars that are still affecting people today."

"Wow, what exactly is post-traumatic stress?" Miguel asked as his palms started to sweat.

The doctor cleared his throat, "Well in layman's terms it is an uncontrollable flashback to the trauma that feels like it is happening in the present."

Miguel drew a sharp breath and felt his pulse spike because he heard machine gunfire to his left. Instinctively, he swerved hard to avoid danger.

With genuine concern for both of them Leon asked "Um, are you all right?"

Pulled back to the present Miguel centered himself and the car as he tried to recover, "My apologies, I think maybe my blood sugar is a bit low. I haven't had a moment to eat today."

The good doctor opened his bag and offered him a Bajadera candy. Miguel accepted the hazelnut treat common in Montenegro and smiled but cringed internally at the lie he told to avoid the ugly truth.

As they arrived at the hotel, the doctor shook Miguel's hand and gave Miguel his business card and another candy.

Leon smiled, "The candy is for your daughter, the card is for you in case you ever need a friend." Miguel was silent with gratitude and thought how ironic it was that Trump characterized all of Leon's people as aggressive after pushing the Montenegrin ambassador out of the way.[ii]

As he saw a twenty-five dollar electronic tip come in a huge smile grew across his face. Given the impersonal nature of paying with an app, tips were not a given. Miguel was always measuring himself against others. He tried to find out if his tips were average or not, but so little data was available. He read in one place that only 35% of people tip Uber drivers all the time. On that metric he was way ahead. Miguel's charm worked in his favor and he almost always received a tip, but they were rarely so generous.[iii]

CHAPTER SIX

Traya and Tano didn't have time to rest on their laurels after completing the human trafficking case. Just as the excitement was finishing up on the live feed with the arrest of the perpetrator, their boss Vinnie entered the room. His formal name was Vincente and he was a third generation child of Catholic immigrants. Vinnie's family experienced firsthand the hatred that bigotry cultivates. His great grandparents were targeted by the KKK when they settled in Indiana after leaving Italy in the 1920s. It was the darker side of American history and not typically taught in school. The dynamic duo worked for Vinny since the early days of the formation of Homeland Security.

Vinny nodded warmly, "Good job guys."

"Thanks boss," the two chimed in with a hair of concern as to why Vinny was really making an in-person congratulations.

The two didn't have to wait long as Vinny got right to business, "So I bet you are wondering what's up next for you guys?"

"A vacation," suggested Tano.

"A raise," added Traya.

"Nice ideas, but I have an opportunity for you. As you know we've been trying to track what 'The Collective' has been up to for years," said Vinnie.

Tano grumbled, "Yeah I always wanted to pin down their illicit financial transactions and ties to Islamic State. Crafty buggers."

"Well now's your chance to put your thumb on the scale of justice and take down Richard Nunn. We've noticed an unusual set of land purchases and think they are making some kind of play," Vinny said enthusiastically.

Richard Nunn was the leader of The Collective. The secretive organization was suspected of seeding Islamic terrorist activities around the world so their various investments would profit. Either he and his cohorts had Jedi-like vision for what land would become valuable or something corrupt had to be afoot.

In the past they were suspected of having a hand in sponsoring Media Titan's development. The program Media Titan was used as a blatant theft of intellectual property over a decade ago when China posted countless television shows and movies online without proper compensation to the appropriate owners. People flocked to the site in droves. In a short period of time Media Titan gained hundreds of millions of users. When Media Titan was breached it caused a financial crisis crippling the credit card industry as well as related financial institutions and small business with the proliferation of stolen personal data. In addition to profiting from their military investments, The Collective invested deeply in identity theft services to benefit from the fear their chaos caused.

Alex was a somewhat unwitting player, having helped the company behind Media Titan dramatically improve the efficiency of their compression algorithms. She had no idea that others planned to exploit Media Titan's user base to inflict havoc on the world. Given that she was complicit in China's brazen IP theft, she was lucky not to have been implicated.

Media Titan was just one of many countless shady ventures The Collective was assumed to have its hands in. While it was suspected that The Collective's financial reach touched every corner of the globe, they left no trail that could be prosecuted.

Vinny called up Memex. The initial research they initiated was correlating purchases from a series of what appeared to be shell companies. 117 straight up purchases were in Canada. Parcels of land ranged from relatively small land grabs to huge ranches. In Greenland, while the obtained lands were not technically purchases, 52 use of land grants were made. Greenland didn't allow the purchase of land, just it's utilization. Other significant sales showed up in Russia and a few scattered across Europe and Patagonia.

Many of the purchases were paid in Bitcoin and other newer digital currencies.

"Interesting, perhaps President Trump was serious about buying Greenland," Traya stated.

"Can you really believe anything our brazen leader says?" Tano added.

"You guys better be careful, you'll end up like Strzok and Page," warned Vinny.[iv]

"Persecuting them for comments most of us were making was ridiculous," Tano responded.

"Everything about the Talking Yam is suspect. How can people not comment? I mean even his 'Make America Great Again' slogan was stolen from Reagan," Traya added.[v]

"We can go all day talking about Trumpisms, I would just advise you guys never to put anything in writing," Vinny said with a fatherly tone. "In the meanwhile, you guys need to track down the common denominator with all of these purchases and verify where the funds are coming from," Vinny commanded with a soft, but firm tone. He was no fan of the hate that bred from the Trump rhetoric, but he had a job to do. Like the vast majority of life-long government employees, he did his job with diligence regardless of his affinity for the administration. It amazed him that a big deal was made about personal chatter between agents. On any sizable case there are agents who liked and disliked any administration.

"On it!" the two said enthusiastically.

CHAPTER SEVEN

After an hour, Alex was released by the medic after resting and receiving fluids. She joined Caidy and they were just in time to catch the awards ceremony. Since it was such a rare occurrence to see someone from Team USA on the podium, even without their cool down clothes, they paused to watch the ceremony.

Alex and Caidy worked through the crowd to get a better look. Jennifer bowed her head in front of a stunning, young local woman who was dressed like a beauty pageant winner. The young lady placed a wreath on Jennifer's head and then the medal around her neck. Alex and Caidy were smiling with a nationalist's pride. Then Alex almost peed herself. Jennifer had doctored her race number. She changed it from 445 to 4445 and added a greater than sign between 44 and 45.

Caidy looked at Alex, "Are you ok?"

It took a minute for Alex to get her composure. "Yes, yes, LOVE Jennifer."

Caidy agreed, "Well yeah, look how well she did."

Alex could tell she didn't get it and wasn't sure she wanted to ruin the joke by explaining it. "I know you went to school when they taught *New Math*, but 44 > 45 only makes sense in one context. One that's going to cause a tweetstorm from our angry creamsicle of a leader."

As the ceremony ended, Alex said goodbye to Caidy and walked to the athlete's tent where she grabbed her equipment bag and could already feel the sense of dread coming over her. Surely her mom would have followed her progress online.

"There's no way they would have shown my collapse on the official race feed," Alex thought confirming to herself that they would be focused on the finish line and not her stumbles out on the course.

Opening up her only official USA bag, one she was given as a member of the USA Junior team, she reached in for her phone. Turning the power back on, she anxiously waited for the Samsung Note 10+ to reboot. In general, she didn't spend her money frivolously, but when it came to computer equipment or phones, she gave into the consumerism plague and always had the latest equipment.

The messages and missed calls were endless. She could see the string of attempts her mom made literally from the minute she dropped on the course.

"OMG, Alex, I hope you are alright," was one text. Yes, even her mother learned to use texting acronyms after all these years of Alex's encouragement.

"Alex it's been two hours, please call," stated another.

There must have been 15 attempts including her mom trying to Skype her. A lot of her friends had iPhones, and thus used FaceTime to chat, but Alex despised Apple's walled-garden approach severely limiting what you can do in their ecosystem. FaceTime only worked for people with Apple devices, which didn't include most of her family and a few very important friends. To her the choice was simple, use software that worked everywhere.

Of course, there was one text from her dad who never misses an opportunity to criticize, and is always direct and to the point, "Call!"

While there were also texts from friends and triple digit notifications from Facebook, Alex decided to rip the proverbial Band-Aid off and reach out to her mom.

Alex called and the phone literally picked up on one ring. "For all that's holy, thank God!" Ann proclaimed.

"I'm fine mom," Alex replied as if she were still in high school.

"What happened honey?"

Alex hated to have to relive her failure, let alone explain it to her mom. "I just had a bad race Mom. No big deal."

Ann wasn't buying her downplay. "Can we get on Skype? I want to see my baby's face."

Ann was the furthest thing from a digital native and normally abhorred technology, but when it came to staying in touch with her daughter, she learned what she needed to in order to keep Alex within reach.

The noticeable pause from Alex told Ann all she needed to know. Alex was hiding something. If Alex hopped on Skype, her mom would see the gash across her nose and forehead that she gave herself when she hit the pavement.

"Sorry Mom, I'd love to, but you know how the Internet is here in Mexico, we'd never get a stable call," Alex said trying to hide her true intentions.

Ann debated whether she should call out her daughter's charade, but she couldn't swallow her *smother* instincts despite remembering Reverend Mongan's advice about not being such a smothering mother.

"Alex, Munse livestreamed the whole thing, given that his race was the day before. I know what happened," Ann said with the concern of a helicopter parent.

Alex was not amused by Munse. *"How much did he really broadcast?"* she wondered to herself.

"Really Mom, it's not that bad," Alex said trying to be convincing.

"I saw you collapse!" shrieked Ann.

"I am sure it looked worse that it was. I just got a little dehydrated. I'm fine now."

Alex knew she needed to move the conversation along and divert it to something else.

"Mom, did you see how well Jennif-" Alex started to say when her father interrupted, "Alex, it's Dad."

"Oh crap," though Alex. On the best of days, Alex's relationship with her dad was a strained one. When Alex had her biggest financial success, getting profits from her contributions to the short-lived Chinese website Media Titan, he condescended to her about how immoral it was to exploit other people's intellectual property for personal gain. It didn't help that over the years, Chinese theft/exploitation of American businesses became an issue that partially led to the current trade war with China. China is notorious for bartering access to their markets with "legal" IP theft.

After an awkward pause, Alex tried to warm the conversation up, "Hi, Dad. How are you?"

"Apparently, better than you are." Alex's dad Charles was never a fan of her race walking. It was a constant distraction to her in school and in his opinion greatly affected her GPA.

"Your mother is too kind to say what really needs to be said."

Alex tried to interject, but whether it was because her dad was hard of hearing or just had selective hearing when on the phone, he just kept barreling along.

"How long are you going to keep this up? It was one thing when you thought you had a future in the sport, but even the best race walkers in the USA make less money than you made on your co-op and you aren't getting any younger." The rant just continued. Alex debated on faking the connection dropping, but knew that would only postpone the inevitable.

"Life isn't all about making money." Alex was getting tired of repeating herself. "Not every Millennial wants to be a FIRE[1]."

"Easy for you to say when you are young and healthy, but what happens when you get older and have nothing saved?" her dad piled on.

"Enough already, I need to go stretch. We can talk when I visit." And with that Alex hung up and noticed a text from her mom.

"Sorry Honey, Dad only wants the best for you."

---

[1] the acronym for Financial Independence Retire Early

CHAPTER EIGHT

After a late night of driving, Miguel woke early. He picked up an aging iPad that was donated to him from Aunt Rosa's friend. He eagerly logged into his bank account to check his latest transactions. It was Monday morning and his weekly take should be waiting for him as Uber typically pays their "employees" every Monday morning with an electronic deposit at 4:00 AM.

Given the time he had to watch his daughter, Miguel only drove 30 hours last week. He always hoped to average more than the ~$20 an hour cited as the industry standard.[vi] Given his kind disposition he usually averaged more when tips were included. "$641.50, not too bad," thought Miguel. However, after expenses which were close to $150 that left money for food and household expenses for the week but not much more.

Given Miguel's legal status, he knew he had a good thing and even though he wanted more, for now this was enough. He had a solid life in Chester, PA thanks to his mother and his Aunt Rosa. Back in 2008, when Miguel was sixteen years of age his mother hired a Coyote to get him across the border so he could live with his aunt.

Coyotes origins trace far back. They were part of an underground system to help illegals cross into the United States when the country was just growing up. Ironically, illegal immigration from Mexico was triggered in the late 1800's when the United States passed laws restricting Chinese and others from immigrating into the country. As the United States further restricted immigration, the need for Coyotes grew.[vii]

A Coyote got him into the country by crossing at the Texas border. After his mom, with the help of his aunt, paid the

$1,000[2] fee to get him out of Mexico, he had to wait in a house with three others for two days. The wait was two-fold; the Coyote needed permission from the Cartel to cross as well as having enough people to make the trip worth the incredible risks associated with crossing the border.[viii]

Ironically, some of the money paid to the Coyote was funneled back to the very people Miguel was trying to escape. The Cartels completely controlled the border. If one person was smuggled across without proper due, the Coyote would be killed. It was not a business for the faint-of-heart.

Miguel had been waiting patiently in a Mexican safe house for what seemed like an eternity. The Coyote said he would tell them when it was time to move. The men thumbed through old magazines and chatted about what they would do once they got to America. There was a nervous energy and a lot of eager anticipation. Around 3pm Hector came to deliver the news that tonight was the night. He unintentionally spit on them as he hissed, "Silence is the key to safe passage and phones are strictly prohibited."

Hector added advice that crossing the border over 100 times without getting caught taught him, "Eat and drink up now because once the crossing is in progress, there would be no stopping until they were across the border."

Miguel ate his stale bread with a Fanta and fanaticized he was eating a slice of pizza in New York.

Just after dark Miguel was loaded with 15 others into a van and driven down a winding road to a river. Hector selected a crossing where the river was lower, where they could just walk

---

[2] It now can cost between $1,200 and $8,000 just to get over the border to a staging area.

across in knee-deep water. He had inflatable rafts in the van just in case the area was heavily patrolled, and they needed to divert to a different location.

Hector barked, "If you fall behind or lose your balance, it's on you. We will not come back for you."

After wading through the swift river, they walked silently on a dirt road. Miguel felt like they may have lost a person along the way, but it wasn't his fight, so he quietly plodded in the cool, dark night. Finally, a new van arrived, picked them up and they were taken to new safe houses in America. The next morning, he was dumped at a Greyhound bus station to fend for himself. From there he went straight to Chester, Pennsylvania.

Miguel rolled over in bed and checked the clock. It was time to get up. Julia, a five-year-old precocious child walked into the bedroom as she rubbed her sleepy eyes and stretched her arms out for a hug. "Come here my coneja! My sweet little bunny."

He brushed her cheek and she broke into a big smile. He met her mother Abigail here in the States while she was studying at West Chester University. Two months into dating, when she found out she was pregnant she told Miguel that she couldn't handle a child right now. Miguel pleaded with her not to have the abortion and she reluctantly agreed, but with one condition. Miguel had to take complete custody and not involve the baby in her life. Julia didn't ask about her mother and was used his aunt being the motherly figure. For now, Miguel did not want to add confusion to her life.

"Papa, can we go to the park and play?" Julia looked him with hope.

"Sorry baby, daddy has to work today."

Julia nodded but her smile faded as the reality set in. Miguel made Julia her favorite heuvos rancheros before heading out. As he set the plate down in front of her, she wagged her finger at him "Aren't you forgetting something?"

Miguel laughed, much to his dismay, Julia's favorite "sauce" was inherited from her mother. He put the bottle of ketchup in front of her and she bobbed her head with approval.

Miguel gave her a kiss on the head before heading out the door. Julia came in for a hug and whispered, "Te amo Papi."

He gave her a squeeze as he fought the tears. He temporarily disabled the Uber on his phone and decided the park was his next destination.

CHAPTER NINE

By the time Alex got off the phone, it was filled with notifications. Jennifer's stunt may have gone unnoticed by Caidy, but the rest of the world picked up on it.

First there were the news articles in her Google feed.

`"American Race Walker Creates Subtle but Frank and Creative Protest on the Podium."`
From CNN

`"Disrespect Again, Liberals Can't Seem to Stand Without a Protest."`
Fox News

`"Why is Race Walking Better for You than Running?"`
RaceWalk.com, recycled an old story to take advantage of the news splash.

USATF released a formal and succinct statement as well. `"Athletes are forbidden to make political protests while representing the USA Track Team. The matter will be looked into and appropriate actions will be taken."`

Then came President Trump's tweets.

The first one was addressed to the incorrect Twitter account, which prompted Jennifer Walker to tweet back, `"tr*mp is really gonna get me to 1k followers eye-."`[ix]

It was quickly corrected and then sent out to the "real" @JenniferRaceWalker.

"Jennifer should never disrespect our Country, the White House, or our Flag, especially since so much has been done for her & the team. Be proud of the Flag that you wear. The USA is doing GREAT!"[x]

What is ironic is that Jennifer was previously quoted as calling President Trump "sexist," "misogynistic," "small-minded," "racist," and "not a good person."[ix] Trump didn't react via social media to the pejorative description of himself.

"Perhaps that was even undeniable for Trump," thought Alex as she walked back to her very convenient hotel. She wasn't staying with the athletes. Instead, she was booked at the equivalent of a Holiday Inn at one end of the racecourse. The hotels the athletes stayed in were reserved solely for the athletes associated with a federation and she wasn't a member of the official team.

As she walked more tweets came in from the general public.

@JenniferRaceWalker, "Jennifer, you want a burger to go with that shake?"

and

@JenniferRaceWalker, "Hey Jennifer, how about a porch to go with that swing? & while u r @ it y don't you leave the USA."

On the USATF Facebook page a thread was highly active with a many people flocking to her support:

BPhillips: In the USA the constitution gives everyone the right to free speech ya know. Go Jennifer! #GirlPower

The only problem for BPhillips was that the constitution doesn't actually protect all forms of speech as was pointed out by one individual that actually studied the constitution. It was highlighted by the following post:

```
Nick Corvera: BPhillips, that sounds nice, but
free speech isn't free. When you work or
represent someone you can't say anything you
want. The first amendment only protects people
from the government prohibiting free speech.
Companies and organizations can do pretty much
what they want.
```

Alex stopped looking at her feeds and headed into her hotel. While she missed her friends, she didn't particularly mind that she had a clean room and a reliable WIFI connection, which she immediately took advantage of and sat down in front of her laptop. At home she had a giant desktop-based system, but on the road, she travelled relatively light. Forget Apple's MacBook's with their flimsy keyboards that frequently break, her road warrior of choice is the HP Spectre 360. While it didn't have the computing power of a gaming laptop, it had a great array of ports so that old and new equipment could be connected to it.

Even better, it had a special privacy screen that was great to hide from peering eyes on a plane or coffee shop. As an added bonus, because the feature was implemented with a screen that refreshed twice as fast as a regular computer screen, it allowed fast motion subjects like race walkers' legs appear smoother in video. Completing her mobile workplace, she also carried a small external USB monitor to give her the room to display much more simultaneously.

Alex fired up her Virtual Private Network to make sure her connection was private and proceeded to check on her work from last night. As much as she hated to admit it, both her dad and Ilia were right even if their reasons conflicted with each other. She had been up late the night before, talking with various friends on online. She used Discord a lot. Discord was the primary communication tool for gamers to talk about their campaigns against other teams. Often in-game chatting is limited for complex coordination. Discord also allowed coordinated conversations between team members to help players get better acquainted. This was the feature Alex really valued. She even met up with more than one virtual friend in the real world.

Other windows she had open were to various adult sex chat sites, job postings in Mexico, and various social media sites like Facebook.

While many studies show that Millennials can't multi-task as well as they think they can, you'd never know that from how many simultaneous conversations Alex maintained.

Alex started with her friend Pedro, who lived only a bus ride from Lázaro Cárdenas. She had been talking with Pedro for almost a year since they met playing in an online game of Star Wars Galaxy of Heroes. He desperately wanted to watch Alex race, but his job wouldn't let him have the day off.

WalkChick: "Hey, I'm done."

DarthDro: "Sorry to hear about your race Alex."

Alex was frustrated by how everyone knew everything and almost immediately.

WalkChick: "It's ok, they'll be other races."

DarthDro: "You looked great."

DarthDro: "At least until you fell 😊"

Alex felt that Pedro had a crush on her. She couldn't count the number of times he requested photos of her. Until she was coming to Mexico, he didn't even know her real name, but she wanted to meet him and hiding that she was racing in the town near him seemed too much to hide.

Once she gave her real name, Pedro quickly connected with her "real" identities on Facebook, Instagram and Twitter. For better or worse, Pedro was now connected to her; maybe a little too much for comfort.

WalkChick: "It wasn't as bad as it probably looked."

WalkChick: "You still want to get together tonight?"

DarthDro: "Is the Pope Catholic? Hell yeah."

WalkChick: "Bring your laptop, we can check out that new game 'The Outer Worlds.'"

DarthDro: "U got it."

Meanwhile in another window Caidy was checking in:

Caidy: "You up for the after party?"

Alex: "I'll make an appearance. Details?"

At larger IAAF events there were formal after race parties. They were a great opportunity for athletes, coaches, the organizers and even media to interact in a relaxed, festive environment. However, the Pan Am Cup was not one of those events. Although many of the athletes assumed there had to be a party somewhere, no one had the details to the non-existent party.

Caidy: "Not sure yet, supposedly it's near where we eat."

Alex: "Let me know when you know. I can't stay long, but I need to let people know I am still alive..."

Back to her conversation with Pedro…

WalkChick: "I have to attend a function for the race, but let's meet up in the hotel lounge at 9PM."

DarthDro: "I'll be there!"

WalkChick: "Sure thing!"

Alex checked emails, responded to a few and then drifted off into a deep post-race slumber.

CHAPTER TEN

"The Collective's reach is infinite," exclaimed Tano in disgust as she looked down at the web-like graphs on her computer screens. Each graph started with the names of shell corporations with recent large land purchases, but no real business activity to justify the purchases. Lines emerged from them to multiple subsidiary corporations. The corporations in turn splintered into a series of bubbles with country names and a series of numbers indicating how many purchases were made as well as the total cost of those purchases. On the bottom was a final number $10,543,250,101, the total amount of transactions suspected of belonging to The Collective.

Traya was staring at an entanglement of his own. His graphs started the same, but ended with individual names, number of transactions and total amounts of money transferred. His number was lower, only $53,521,300. Traya peered over to look at Tano's total and admitted, "Well you've got me beat."

The duo worked together, along with a team of young, super savvy computer experts that helped gather much of the original data and continued to feed them with more data every day. One of them, Caroline Peters, was a recent graduate from University of Maryland's Computer Science department. While not as well-known as MIT or Stanford's programs, their graduates were top notch.

"Guys, I have something interesting for you to look at. I've been plotting the recent land grabs against a 2D world map," said Caroline.

She pulled Tano's keyboard over saying, "Let me drive."

Her fingers danced on the keyboard and reconfigured the monitor to show her findings. The globe had two horizontal bands of red dots running across it. Each one circled close to the Earth's poles.

We've all been so focused on the sources we missed the obvious.

"Clearly The Collective has a plan," Traya declared.

Tano concluded, "So they are smart enough to go after all the resources opening up from global warming."

"But I thought 'conservatives' like the members of The Collective didn't believe in climate change," questioned Caroline.

"Conservatism is certainly a flexible term. How many steadfast conservative values went by the wayside when President Trump grabbed the reigns of the Republican party? Besides, many conservatives have evolved from being abject climate change deniers to simply denying that it's caused by man," Traya explained.

"Look at Traya the historian, you going to start spewing how climate change is all due to the Milankovitch cycles," sarcastically challenged Tano. Both agents were avid environmentalists. Their passion for the environment had made them fast friends. They were horrified by the lack of commitment paid to the effects of climate change.

Caroline looked at Tano curiously, "What the hell is a Milanksomething cycle?"

"It's what they didn't teach you at school. It's a series of cycles the Earth iterates through that effect the amount of solar radiation that the Earth absorbs. The cycles lead to changes in climate, but usually over tens of thousands of years. Climate change deniers have tried to hijack the theory as an explanation for the dramatic changes in climate that have happened recently. With the US pulling out of the Paris climate accord and not exploring safe nuclear energy, the writing is pretty much on the wall," lectured Traya.

"Well, whatever The Collective believes about climate change isn't exactly a crime. It is puzzling though that they are climate change deniers and are buying land that will only be valuable if climate change isn't reversed."

"True, but we know better than to think everything is on the up and up. I don't doubt The Collective isn't behind the lack of progress in nuclear power. It's really the answer to reducing greenhouse gas emissions," Traya explained.

"What do you mean, with accidents like Fukushima how can you call nuclear power safe?" asked Caroline.

"Well it's not that black and white. Plants like Fukushima were designed in the 1960's. That was before we used computers for such tasks. They were literally designed with a slide-rule. Would you even drive a car that was designed that way? The new nuclear plants are super-efficient and uses fuel completely differently than a traditional nuclear power plant."

Bill Gates' company TerraPower claims to have figured out how to use radioactive waste from the standard uranium enrichment process as fuel for the new reactor. Given that the US has over 700,000 metric tons of depleted uranium, on paper it could power the needs of the entire planet for more than a million years.[xi]

Caroline felt like she was back in school, "If it's so great, then why isn't he building it?"

"That's one place where the environmentalists have shot themselves in the foot. Too many regulations have prevented any new nuclear power plants from being developed in the USA," continued Traya.

"Well that sucks," a frustrated Caroline concluded.

CHAPTER ELEVEN

Alex woke to her phone ringing, it was Caidy.

"Hey Caidy," Alex answered, still half asleep.

"Sleepy head, it's time to go out. There's no after party, but we are all going dancing at the Bandidos club and we're leaving in five minutes."

One might think that after a long-distance race, the last thing you'd want to do is dance. However, given the hard-disciplined days of training, the night after a race was one of the rare times elite athletes get to go out like normal people. Some told themselves it was good to get the muscles loose and get that lactic acid out, but it was really an excuse to drink, relax and, all too often, to hook up. While it's not part of the gear highlighted on social media, the Olympic athletes are provided with a plentiful supply of condoms. At the previous winter Olympics over 100,000 condoms were distributed!

"OK, I'll make it."

Alex quickly cleaned up and headed out the door. The streets which had been closed for the race were now open to traffic. Walking along the "sidewalk," she went flying for the second time today. The walkways were like a war zone, broken apart and incredibly uneven. The contrast to the racecourse, that was clearly repaved just for the race, was dramatic. Her ego was bruised more than her body, but it was a reminder she needed to keep aware of her surroundings.

With the sun setting, most of the businesses along the street were closed and shuttered up with graffiti-filled aluminum doors pulled over the storefronts. The streetlights which illuminated the roads, didn't quite reach the sidewalks, and even at her slow, post-race pace, she had to walk carefully. When the racecourse was set up, she never noticed the surroundings, because she was able to just walk down the main road.

She approached the club which had curtains pulled over the front where walls or windows would be. The salsa music pulsed out with a ferocity that could shake a building to the ground.

Alex never liked loud music, but her friends were much more adventurous than she was and would frequent far more rambunctious places than were in her comfort zone. Once inside, she could see the large dance floor that consumed the majority of the establishment. There was a small bar on one side of the room and in the corners were a few spartan tables where a bunch of locals who looked like cowboys who just got off a ranch were sitting.

Alex saw Caidy, Munse, Jennifer and a few other race walkers huddled at the bar. They were the only non-locals there. Fresh juice drinks appeared to be the specialty, but many were also drinking a local beer, Noche Buena. Alex looked at the bottle, 5.9% ABV. *"Geez, someone is looking for some liquid courage,"* thought Alex.

The bar was so excited to have competitors from the Caminata that they made an enthusiastic announcement over the music. "It's not every day that we get visitors from the United States, but today we are lucky to have competitors from today's race. Welcome them!" then a large, raucous cheer filled the bar.

The bartender bought out a beer for each of the race walkers and said, "On the house."

This was exactly the kind of place US track team's staff would tell the team to avoid. The US athletes thought it was a magical experience.

Munson approached Alex, "Hey Alex, sorry about intruding earlier."

"It's ok," even though she didn't mean it.

"Let me make a peace offering. Here are all the photos and some videos from your race," handing Alex a USB stick while smiling, knowing she couldn't resist. What millennial doesn't like photos of themselves?

Alex grabbed her beer when behind the curtains the clang of the metal doors coming down could be overheard.

All the athletes looked at each other in astonishment. *"Maybe this place wasn't such a good choice after all,"* thought Alex.

Then the lights began to dim, the salsa music faded, and a man a bit past his prime, with a bit of a pot belly, emerged. He had a giant sombrero, pitch black eyebrows and mustache and an ornate black suit. He was a Vicente Fernandez impersonator, the equivalent of Mexico's Elvis Presley.

While there was a degree of local charm, Alex knew she had to meet up with Pedro and excused herself for the evening while the rest of the athlete's enjoyed the show and Lord knows what else.

CHAPTER TWELVE

Miguel scrolled through photos of his daughter playing in the park to see what he wanted to post on Facebook. They were so much happier now that they had moved from Chester, PA to Wallingford. Wallingford was only 20 minutes away but provided low income housing without the threats of bullets flying or drugs moving through the area.

Two years ago, the decrepit barracks were refurbished by the state to create clean stand-alone houses with small porches. There is a lot to be said for hot water and plumbing that works on a regular basis. Miguel's aunt was fortunate enough to be able to acquire a USDA mortgage without even needing to put in a down payment. With Miguel helping to pay a portion of the monthly payment, it was a great situation for all of them.

Now instead of worrying about every loud sound that popped off in the distance, they could play in the park. Admittedly, it wasn't much of a park by many people's standards, but it was a safe green space where kids could swing, climb on the jungle gym and fly a kite.

The park was Miguel's special place to spend time with Julia. At least once a week they went to watch the clouds and identify them as to the animals they resembled. It was also a great time for Miguel to reinforce Julia's Mexican roots. Miguel would let Julia call out the animal first. Then Miguel would recite to her the Spanish word and make her repeat it.

Sometimes at night they would go to star gaze and Miguel would point out the Big Dipper, Little Dipper and Orion's belt. Julia always laughed when Miguel said Big Dipper, which made her think of an ice cream cone.

During the day, they would wander the perimeter looking for IDK's. IDK's were something that was an "I don't know." They delighted in finding prehistoric caterpillars, man eating moths, and of course the ever-reclusive mole. His daughter had his love of the unknown and he created stories to explain things.

Julia was also a philosopher of sorts. At the tender age of three Julia looked at Miguel in the middle of discussion about why she couldn't have what she wanted and said, "Well, I guess it is what it is Daddy." Miguel tried to carry this philosophy forward in his daily life. He did what he could for his family, but let go of what he couldn't control. He tried to be a valuable member of the community and show appreciation for the opportunities provided to him.

At first when Miguel saw the signs "Hate Has no Home Here" he felt welcomed. The message was repeated in multiple languages including Spanish. Soon after, the ubiquitous sign had company. "Love Lives Here" signs started sprinkling across conservative lawns. This was the Trump lovers' answer to what some viewed as an attack on conservative values.

A cursory glance implies the "Loves Lives Here" sign is innocuous and kindhearted. However, it was really a veiled message denying prejudice by people who primarily voted for a president who constantly spews racisms and division. Instead of a wonderful sign encouraging acceptance and tolerance, "Love Lives Here" hailed the right of American's to protect their love ones from anyone who might bring instability to their comfortable little nest by being different.[xii]

Miguel found the best photo of Julia pointing up at a bird flying over the park and uploaded that to Facebook with the caption "Nature is a great adventure." With that Miguel placed his phone on the charger and drifted off to a sound sleep.

Miguel awoke to the sounds of people shouting next door. *"Damn it, those two need to break up already,"* he thought as he looked over at the clock. *"4AM? What are they doing up this early anyway?"*

It didn't take long to realize this wasn't the repeated argument his neighbors had when Andrew came home drunk. There were other voices in the mix.

"We are from ICE. We are here under the authority of the Illegal Immigration Reform and Immigrant Responsibility Act. Let us in," he heard. Miguel sat petrified in fear. Immigration and Customs Enforcement (ICE) raids were the specter that haunted the nights of every undocumented immigrant.

Previously ICE targeted the workplace, rounding up numerous undocumented workers in a single sweep. However, in recent years, especially under the Trump administration, the focus shifted. Now ICE targets people in their houses, usually at the wee hours of the morning when they know most people will be home.

In the past, immigrants like Miguel had less to fear. Law abiding undocumented workers were not targeted. However, in 2017 when Thomas Homan, the acting director of ICE declared, "You should be uncomfortable. You should look over your shoulder," every illegal immigrant no longer slept with both eyes shut.

Now, anyone could be targeted. Low-income communities with many families living in proximity were common targets. *"Would they be coming for him?"* he wondered.

He didn't have to wait long for his answer. A loud pounding ensued on their front door. "Miguel Lopez, this is ICE. Open the door," shouted the officer.

He froze for a moment, but then sprang into action. His aunt was already up, but somehow sound sleeper that Julia was she was still out cold. As he approached the door, he signaled to his Aunt Rosa to go to Julia's room. Fortunately, she had prepared them for this day. He knew his rights.

Miguel tried to sound confident, "Do you have a warrant?"

There was a noticeable pause, "Miguel don't make this harder on yourself. Of course, we have a warrant."

"I am not opening this door until you show it to me," countered Miguel.

"Just come out here and we'll show it to you," implored the officer.

"I don't think so, slip it under the door."

The wait seemed interminable, but within seconds, to his horror a piece of paper came through the crack at the bottom of the door. To his surprise it was a warrant and it did have his name on it.

"We did what you asked now open up Miguel, do you want us to damage your aunt's door?"

Miguel was shocked. They knew enough about him that they knew he lived with his aunt. "What else did they know," he thought to himself.

Miguel felt his heart racing as his eyes tried to cover the legalese of the document when he remembered the advice of the pro bono lawyer he and his aunt met with after Trump was elected and put fear in every immigrant's daily life. Miguel scanned down to find the signature on the warrant. "Got ya," he thought.

"What are you trying to pull, this isn't signed by a judge, just some immigration office named Whinston LaPierre," Miguel replied with a little bit of confidence.

The officer was ready for this defense. Whether immigrants got legal advice, or they just educated themselves on the Internet more and more weren't intimidated by their simple tactics. ICE knew how to play the game as well and continued the pressure. "It doesn't matter Miguel; you are here illegally. If you don't come with us, we'll arrest your aunt and your daughter will be remanded into foster care. Is that what you want?"

Hitting Miguel's Achilles heel, they had him. Aunt Rosa came out of the back room. "No Miguel, you can't."

He hugged his aunt and Miguel whispered, "Por favor protégela." He prayed his aunt would be able to protect his daughter from what was about to come and then opened the door.

CHAPTER THIRTEEN

Alex headed back to the motel and rushed to her room. Knowing Pedro was on his way, she wanted to download the images/videos from the thumb drive onto her computer. She also copied a small program from her computer onto the drive before slipping it back in her pocket.

She finished just in time, as Pedro texted that he was downstairs.

Pedro appeared a lot like his Facebook's timeline portrayed him. In his late twenties, with jet black dark hair, he wasn't very fit, but stylishly dressed. He carried a small bag, holding his laptop. His warm smile was apparent the moment his eyes connected with Alex's. He spoke English extremely well as he lived in the United States as an undocumented worker for almost ten years before getting deported a year ago in an ICE raid.

"Alex, it's so good to meet you in person," Pedro said.

Alex gave him a friendly hug and directed him into the bar area.

"That was some race today!" Pedro stated looking for something to break the ice. Sure, they'd known each other online for a while, but they never actually spoke, or even video chatted. It had the awkward feel of a blind date, even though Alex never gave him a hint of a romantic possibility. Still, as a single guy, he did fantasize about his American friend. *"If she married me, could I go back to the States?"* he thought.

"I'm glad you missed it, how was work?"

"Work," Pedro paused, "is well, work." He didn't talk much about his work. For those deported from the USA, finding work was difficult. Many worked in call centers just over the border with US and Mexican-based companies exploiting the poor souls kicked out of the USA when they were most vulnerable.

With Pedro's family deep inside Mexico, it didn't make sense for him to stay near the border. Fortunately, he had been sending money back to his family while working in the States, so they had money to help him get resettled. Because of his strong language abilities and reasonable computer skills he was able to get a job working for a US-based advertising agency. Jobs weren't just outsourced to China; Mexico had a healthy set of opportunities.

"Work is a four-letter word, at least in English," Alex joked.

They ordered a couple of drinks and then Alex offered, "Hey, since you missed the race, do you want a bunch of photos and videos one of the USA team members took of me?"

How could Pedro say no? Alex slightly worried about what he might do with all the photos in private, but shared anyway. Pedro quickly snatched the USB drive, powered on his laptop, and copied the contents into a folder.

Alex took back the thumb drive, as a text came in on her phone.

001701: Connection Established.

Alex smiled to herself. *"Mission accomplished,"* she thought.

Their drinks came and Alex paid without giving Pedro a chance to offer. Pedro wasn't an experienced dater. He definitely wasn't used to an attractive woman buying him drinks.

"You didn't have to do that Alex."

"No worries, it's all good," Alex raised her beer to his.

They drank their beers and chit chatted. As they were close to finishing their beers, Pedro suggested, "Let's check out that game."

"Sure thing," Alex pulled out her laptop as well.

Pedro ordered two more beers. *"I guess beer being liquid courage is an international concept,"* thought Alex. He was clearly hoping the night didn't end with just a video game.

They both had preinstalled the game and double-clicked to open the program. As the game stepped through the booting process, an all too familiar message popped up on the screen:

`"There is no Internet connection…"`

"Hijo de puta," cursed Pedro.

"I hate to say it, but it is Mexico. These things happen. Hopefully, it will pop back on soon."

Their beers arrived and they continued to make small talk as Pedro incessantly retried his Internet connection to no avail. While Alex would enjoy playing the game, she had accomplished her main goal and didn't really need the night to continue. She drank down her beer as quickly as she could without being obvious.

When she finished hers, it was obvious Pedro was milking his drink to buy him more time. He wasn't taking chances though and signaled the bartender to come over.

Alex, protested, "I'd love to, but the race totally killed me today. I'm definitely over my limit and I had one with the team before I met you. I think I need to call it a night."

A dejected Pedro really couldn't argue. "I understand," he mumbled like a grade schoolboy crushed by his first love. It didn't help matters that Alex was scheduled to fly back to the States the next morning. So much for his fantasies, but at least he had a slew of photos and videos.

"A quick selfie," he asked?

"Of course!" Alex slid over, put an arm around him as he held out his cell phone for the stereotypical shot.

Alex said goodnight and then headed up for bed. She wasn't just heading back home. Instead, she used the trip as an excuse to fly to see her parents. While she lived close enough to visit more often, it had been a long time since she had seen them. Unfortunately, while she lived within a few hours' drive, their stressed relationship led to few visits.

CHAPTER FOURTEEN

As Miguel stepped out of the safe haven of his aunt's home, he was swung around quickly by an officer and handcuffed. "Let's go," the officer barked.

They walked to the van and he was roughly shoved into the back with a slew of other detainees. The drive out to York County Detention Center, which was also a local prison, was a quiet and somber affair. Everyone in the back of the van knew what fate awaited them. Given Trump's vitriol there was little hope for undocumented immigrants.

The non-descript red brick building proudly flew a United States flag high above. Miguel looked up at it and prayed that this wasn't goodbye.

The line of detainees was led into the building and dumped in brick room with a drain in the middle of the floor. Given the hour of his arrest and his abrupt awakening he had few belongings to confiscate. His cellphone and wallet were all he had. They were placed in a plastic bag and sent to the office.

"Take your clothes off and face the wall."

Miguel hesitantly complied with the demand. He was stripped searched, including a very uncomfortable probe of his cavities. This was followed by a rough hose down and shower of anti-lice powder. As they led Miguel to his cell, Miguel remembered the training he had been given by his aunt in case he was ever arrested. Miguel hesitantly stated, "I'm entitled to a phone call."

"Later," was the terse response from the rotund guard anxious to get back to texting his girlfriend who was on a double shift at the hospital. These early morning raids aggravated him to no end as this shift was supposed to be quiet.

As the door clinked and closed Miguel felt the bile rise in his throat. He didn't know if he should cry or scream in anger. He had tried so hard. With the exception of entering the USA illegally, once here, he was a completely law-abiding person. He was building a life for Julia and himself and now he sat in prison as an ICE detainee.

He knew his aunt would visit as soon as she could find him, but he had no idea how long that might be. Miguel looked around the unwelcoming room. Two lumpy beds and bare brick walls led out to a common area with lots of tables. This was his new home.

From the common room he heard a voice, "How did they get you? Did they threaten your family too?" Miguel was startled by the man who had been eyeing him since he arrived.

Miguel walked out and took a seat, "They threatened my aunt and daughter. Name's Miguel by the way."

"Lo Siento, you lose your social etiquette in here after a while. I'm Rodrigo and your new cell mate. They got me by threating to prosecute my brother who is here and has a green card. He had too many outstanding traffic and parking tickets and they said they would put him away if I didn't cooperate. You're lucky, your aunt and kid are innocent so you may be able to use the threat in court to your advantage. I bet having a kid is a big plus." Like many undocumented immigrants Rodrigo didn't really know what would or wouldn't help someone's case.

Miguel nodded thinking that he didn't see his daughter as an advantage only a sweet child who would be confused and asking questions that his aunt had no good answers for. Rodrigo tossed him a magazine and chuckled, "Here, housewarming gift." Miguel looked at the cover of the Time Magazine. Trump was on the cover, glowing with pomposity and an artificial orange hue that Trump attributes to "the light's no good. I always look orange."[xiii]

Seeing that "Puto Naranjo" turned his stomach and Miguel promptly tossed it back.

Rodrigo shook his head, "I didn't give it to you to read. I thought you might want to use it as toilet paper." They both laughed but at the same time it was hard not to feel rage growing deep inside him.

CHAPTER FIFTEEN

Six in the morning wasn't the ideal time for Charles and Ann to make a trip to Philadelphia's airport, but Alex's connection red-eyed from the west coast and they weren't about to tell her to Uber back to Medford, NJ. Philadelphia's airport is a mess under the best of circumstances; they sat in the cell phone lot until Alex texted she landed.

Alex traveled relatively light; she avoided carrying checked bags at all costs. Like many, she packed her carry-on to capacity. However, she had a little trick that worked out great over the years. She wore a "luggage" jacket. It looked like a normal jacket, but it had large compartments she could place clothing and various pieces of electronics. On one trip she weighed it full. It held just over twenty pounds of gear.

As she approached the lengthy, serpentine lines herding travelers through customs she chuckled a little to herself at their plight. Alex had the forethought to sign up for Global Entry, which for a few dollars more than TSA Pre-check allowed her to bypass the time-consuming system of customs processing. Instead, she zipped through customs without waiting in long lines.

She quickly texted her parents to pull up as she made for the exit. Half race walking, half pedestrian walking she blazed through the airport with Olympic-like efficiency passing the long line of disgruntled passengers waiting to get through the initial customs checkpoint and the even larger group waiting for their bags.

Alex managed to exit the airport just as her parents pulled up. The relatively, cooler drier air was a relief from the oppression in Mexico. She popped in the back seat and greeted her parents warmly. "Thanks Mom and Dad!"

"Great to have you home," her mom replied with a warm smile.

"Likewise," was about all her dad could muster.

Both parents were dressed in their Sunday best and as this dawned on Alex, she realized the ride wasn't for free. She knew exactly where they were headed. "Dad I don't suppose you would drop me off at home? It's not far out of the way."

Her dad wasn't about to forgo an easy opportunity for a family outing to church. "Sorry honey, you know we like to go to the early service."

She tried a last ditch effort, "But Dad, I'm not dressed for church."

"The Lord won't judge you for your clothing choice," her dad said in a tone that she knew she lost the argument.

Alex pondered making a sarcastic quip related to the Old Testament's restriction against wearing clothing of mixed materials, she gave up.

When Alex was in college her friend David worked on an archeological dig that uncovered artifacts whose allegations against Christianity helped derail attendance. Once the artifacts were proven fraudulent, church attendance improved dramatically. Now, the pews were typically full for multiple services every Sunday. Reverend Mongan however always kept seats open for his most loyal parishioners, the Pintos.

Alex hated sitting upfront, but she had no choice. The lack of sleep, exhaustion from the race and general lack of interest in the service, led her to slip in and out of consciousness.

Alex popped awake. Whether it was from coincidence, her subconscious screaming at her, or perhaps it was her dad kicking her awake she didn't know. What she did know was she felt nauseous as she heard the last of the sermon. "And we must all bless President Trump for the hard work he is doing to make America great again. His tireless efforts supporting conservative values are unequaled in modern times."

The anger within Alex was ready to explode. Alex did all she could to not jump out of her chair and rail against Reverend Mongan.

As a child, while she didn't buy the Christian doctrine he was selling, she did appreciate his kind heart and generous demeanor. It was apparent to her that he was seduced by the dark side as well.

"Wasn't he a 'Never Trumper' when the election started?" she wondered to herself.

It amazed her how one Never Trumper after another was entrapped by the power Trump wielded. The worst was Senator Lindsey Graham who had called Trump a "kook", "crazy" and "unfit for office" during the campaign. [xiv] However, after the election he was quoted complimenting the president by saying ""I personally like him. We play golf. He's very nice to me."

Of course, there was also Mitt Romney, who pulled no punches saying "His is not the temperament of a stable, thoughtful leader. His imagination must not be married to real power," as well as "His promises are as worthless as a degree from Trump University." [xv] But now that Trump has a stranglehold on the Republican Party, Romney usually steers clear of criticizing the president simply stating that he won't endorse anyone in 2020.[xvi] When he does criticize him, he will criticize the behavior but not support directly support actions like impeachment against Trump. Instead, he simply states that Trump "is wrong and appalling."[xvii]

The service ended and they made their way to the car. Ann was in the front seat and fastened her safety belt for what was sure to be a figuratively long ride. Getting out of church was actually a chore waiting for the piles of cars to trickle out of the lot. Unfortunately, for Ann this usually meant a father/daughter debate about what was said in the sermon. Today was no exception.

Alex popped in the back and as soon as the car door closed Alex started in, "Dad, I know you voted for him, but you can't possibly support Reverend Mongan preaching that Trump's presidency is the will of God."

"Alex, you have such a limited view of the world. How is Trump any different than the Persian King Cyrus that helped the Israelites move to Palestine and build the second temple? God used Cyrus as a vessel just as he is using Trump," her dad countered.

Even after all these years, she was astonished how often she was surprised by her dad's ability to rationalize and quote the most esoteric examples from the bible. "You could use that argument to say that the ends always justify the means, that's just ridiculous."

Trump's presidency has baffled more than just Alex. Trumpfatigue, was a new syndrome sure to be classified as a new mental disorder for the effects of the constant, easily verifiable lies that came from our commander and chief.

"Jesus would never kick out the homeless and the poor that hobble across our border," Alex piled on.

Her dad had all the standard lines ready, "A country has to have its sovereignty."

"Allowing people to claim asylum is not only what Jesus would do, it's international law. Your problem is you only watch that one station Dad!"

Alex was a media-omnivore and always prided herself on getting her news from all sources. Even before curated news feeds were the norm on cellphones, she had written scripts to gather news stories on topics of interest from all the major outlets. On some days, she'd have the websites of all the major news networks open on a monitor and be dumbfounded that they were reporting on the same stories.

Sometimes there were blatant misrepresentation of the facts, but more often it was very selective curation of the stories. A controversy for a liberal leader was sure to be the headlines on Fox News, while stories about Trump's daily lack of reality were not.

"The rest of those stations are all fake news," quipped her dad.

"Do you remember who invented fake news?" Alex then answered her own question, "Cinnamon Hitler himself."

Alex didn't give her dad time to reply, "Do you remember when Trump said and I quote, 'I have people that have been studying Obama's birth certificate and they cannot believe what they're finding', funny how we never heard what those people found?"

"Every politician has a gaff or two, look at Uncle Joe!"

"All mistakes are not morally equivalent, and you know that. Sure, Biden has misspoken from time to time, but you'll never hear him say anything as bad as 'Grab 'em by the pussy.' or brag about going after married women."[xviii]

"Well the Bible may disagree with you Alex. The bible states in Romans 6:23, 'For the wages of sin is death …'"

"Part of your problem is that you are so closed minded. You know there's actually a Christian textbook out there that preaches keeping a closed mind to live a Christ-pleasing life. What are Christians so afraid of?"[xix]

Charles was tired of the game, but also one not to back down. "You're the one that is closed minded. Did you ever give President Trump a chance?"

"He started lying on the first day. Need I remind you about crowd sizes? What's he compensating for? Maybe those small hands?"

Alex didn't wait for a reply. "The number of 'Pants on Fire' quotes Orangehole makes a day is mind numbing. What was it the other day he said, 'the first lady has gotten to know Kim Jong-Un and I think she would agree with me, he is a man with a country that has tremendous potential?'[xx] Except, that she never met him."

"The thing that's so intolerable is he doesn't just lie about facts that can't be checked; he constantly lies about easily verifiable facts." Then Alex decided to play by her dad's rules, "Doesn't the bible say that God does not accept a person who practices deceit, Psalm 101:7."

Ann had her limit, so she turned on the car radio to attempt to stop the conversation.

"The searing reprimand of former FBI director James Comey by a Justice Department Inspector General is only the start of a series of blows to the reputations of key law enforcement figure," blasts out, Ann wasn't thinking since Fox News was their default and only setting for the radio *dial*.

"Why are you guys so obsessed with Comey? I bet the next story will be on Clinton's emails, or should they cover Trump tweeting about how the Clinton's are behind Jeff Epstein's death? Perhaps they should cover how many of the people he surrounds himself with are all criminals? Didn't President Trump say he would bring in the best and brightest people? Instead he brought a clan of people who now have a ton of indictments."

"So, Alex, why don't you tell us more about your race?" Ann switched the topic.

CHAPTER SIXTEEN

"A person often meets his destiny on the road he took to avoid it," was one of French poet Jean de La Fontaine's most famous quotes. Richard Nunn, head of The Collective was forced to recite dribble like that when studying in the stodgy prep school his parents made him attend as a child. He didn't believe in relinquishing control then and certainly didn't now. Nunn was a control freak; he didn't leave details to chance. Now was no exception.

Upon hearing the news, he immediately called his Chinese counterpart Shen Lei. The pair had collaborated for more than a decade since he brought Lei into the group after the Media Titan effort. Lei proved useful not just opening Chinese markets to The Collective's international businesses, but he was instrumental in helping craft Chinese policies that could be effective for The Collective's enterprises.

"Shen, it's been too long," Nunn greeted his friend. As always, Nunn had his trademark cigar twirling through his fingers.

Shen tolerated the cigar's stench at far too many meetings and was glad this conversation was over a web conference. "Indeed, it has Richard. To what do I owe the pleasure?"

"Shen, we have a problem."

"Don't you mean an opportunity?"

Nunn laughed, indeed, creating chaos led to many profitable ventures over the years. "Well, this time we need to stop that ridiculous do-gooder, Bill Gates. And to think he used to be as ruthless of a businessman as the best of us!"

When Gates was building his empire, he stopped at nothing to crush the competition. While no one could prove it, he was often thought to have orchestrated changes in DOS such that they broke his competition's software. Microsoft engineers were even so bold as to hide an Easter egg in Excel that played an animation of a Lotus 1-2-3 icon leaving bugs on the screen, only to have an Excel icon swoop in and save the day. Eventually, it caught up with Microsoft as they were successfully sued for antitrust violations in 2001.

"Which of his many ventures has you riled up?" Shen questioned. When Gates refocused his energies, he left the computer world for more philanthropic efforts. Much like some of the biggest robber barons on the early 20th century, after amassing his fortune he turned his wealth to help society. Some of Gate's biggest successes were in cleaning up sanitation in third world counties as well as trying to eradicate polio.

"This idea of creating a safe nuclear power plant," answered Nunn.

"There's no such thing as a safe nuclear plant," Shen contradicted him.

"Well Gates has other ideas. They think they can use existing spent nuclear fuel and feed it to a redesigned power plant without having the risk of a meltdown. From what I read it has a pretty good chance of working."

Shen knew better than to question Nunn too hard. While he was a member of The Collective, there was definitely a pecking order and he was not on top. "How can I help from China with this problem?"

Nunn of course already knew what he wanted. "The environmental laws in the USA are way too restrictive, even under President Trump, to allow a prototype to be developed in a timely and cost-effective manner. That old coot wants to see the fruition of his efforts before he is too old to appreciate it. China is the answer."

With the looser environmental laws and cheap labor, building the prototype in China was a simple answer to the dilemma. Once online and generating power, the world would see the new power plant as the only truly scalable solution to greenhouse gas emissions. Power generation would be carbon neutral.

"I will have to call in many favors. Mr. Gates has a strong influence here, but I understand the significance and it shall be done," pledged Shen.

"I trust it will. Thank you Shen," and with that Nunn terminated the call.

CHAPTER SEVENTEEN

Pedro met up with his friend Alejandro after work. Alejandro was another deportee who was kicked out about a year before Pedro. They each ordered a beer and sat in the corner.

When the bartender brought the beers, Pedro also ordered a double shot of tequila. "It's going to be one of those nights I guess?" asked Alejandro.

Pedro's somber mood was plastered all over his face. "Looks that way," replied Pedro.

"Guess I am not as much to look at as your American girlfriend, am I?" asked Alejandro.

"Not even close, look," Pedro said as he shared the selfie they took.

"Bet you saw a lot more than that smile last night," egged Alejandro.

Angrily, Pedro replies, "I told you nothing happened." Alejandro was much better looking that Pedro. Pedro was always jealous of Alejandro's luck with women.

Alejandro wasn't about to take no for an answer, "I know you don't like to kiss and tell, but she's back in the States, you can spill it."

"Seriously, I have no love life and a crappy job," Pedro complained.

"Who are you complaining to? At least you don't have to work with the public, let alone the American public." Alejandro worked for a call center offering anything from *complementary* vacations to questionable automobile warrantees.

In contrast, Pedro just worked writing fake news and posting it around the Internet under various pseudonyms. Pedro countered, "True, but at least you get to talk to people."

Alejandro wasn't buying it, "Yeah if you call people cursing at you all day talking. People don't exactly care to have their privacy invaded day and night."

Pedro was far more sensitive than his friend. "Sometimes I feel bad about creating so much crap, but how else can I get a decent paying job? Do you ever feel bad about what you do?" asked Pedro.

"Are you kidding me? They kicked us out of their country; not to mention how many countries have they exploited? Those assholes will sell out any country and exploit any worker just to save a nickel for their latest iPhone. They get everything they deserve." Alejandro downed the rest of his beer without pausing for a breath.

"True, but when I lived there, I met a lot of really nice, caring people."

"How nice was the guy that arrested you or the judge that deported you? Did you hear they are now deporting people with valid passports?" Alejandro said.[xxi]

Looking stunned, Pedro replied, "What?"

"Yeah that Orange son-of-a-bitch is obsessed with the notion of a fake birth certificate. First Obama and now anyone with darker skin than his, which isn't that easy given his effervescent Cheeto glow," explained Alejandro.

"That can't be right, is there no limit to what this guy will do to distract people?"

"The government claims that there has been no change in policy, but the numbers speak for themselves. Some are even veterans. Can you imagine if you fought for the USA and then were kicked out?" explained Alejandro.

"I'd be pissed for sure."

"That's why I don't care if what I do is annoying or dishonest. As an imperialist nation they exploited how many third-world countries? Now, with the power of the Internet we can exploit back."

Pedro debated if he should share the latest project at work. Perhaps the shots loosened his inhibitions, perhaps it was just his frustrations. The project was supposed to be confidential and he really didn't know much of the details. "Who would Alejandro tell?" thought Pedro. Then he just blurted it out, "You don't know the half of what's coming."

"What do you mean?"

"Our latest fake news campaign isn't just going to be a controversial meme or two to create angst like the one about Clinton being involved in human trafficking via DC restaurants. It's going to include something called deep fakes."

"What the hell is that?"

"It's when they use computers to make people look like other people. They can literally create fake videos of people talking. Idiots in the USA won't bother checking that what's being said isn't true. Can you imagine when the videos come out of Clinton saying to destroy the emails or Obama admitting his birth certificate was a fake? They'll just repost it on Facebook or retweet it thinking they are so superior and that their side is right, and the other side is evil. They're all evil."

Alejandro wasn't fazed by Pedro's admission, "Ha, I've seen that stuff. It's all over the porn sites. They take famous actresses and put their faces on naked bodies having sex. I always thought it was really cool. I might have seen one or two of Selena Gomez."

"Ha, I bet Justin Bieber has checked them out as well. The porn industry once again has led the technological way." Few people know how much of the technological standards that affect their daily lives were set due to the porn industry. It's an industry whose smutty fingerprints go back to the 1800s. First they set the home film video standard with 8mm cameras. But their influence continued during the war of the video tape formats. Sony was the clear leader in quality with its Betamax format, but they didn't want to allow pornography. The world spoke and VHS was crowned the winner. History repeated itself with Blu-Ray winning over HD DVDs for similar reasons. However, it wasn't just video formats dirtied by porn's smutty fingerprints. Online payments and video streaming all have been strongly influenced by the needs of the porn industry.[xxii]

CHAPTER EIGHTEEN

Miguel and Rodrigo became fast friends. "How long have you been here", Miguel asked Rodrigo.

"It's been a week, but my hearing is tomorrow. I have a guy arranging everything," Rodrigo replied.

"Oh, you have a lawyer?" Miguel questioned with a bit of optimism. *"Perhaps he could recommend a good one,"* Miguel thought to himself.

"He said he's a notario publico and that he would take care of everything. My family gave him like $500," explained Rodrigo.

"That's not good. A notario publico isn't a lawyer and they can't represent you. My aunt was very clear that you shouldn't go near them. Did he actually say he would be in court with you?"

Rodrigo stared back with a fearful silence.

"My aunt sat me down after the election, and reviewed a YouTube video with me on everything we should do in a case like this. Maybe when my aunt gets me a lawyer, he can help you as well?"

Rodrigo looked mortified. "We don't have any more money. We gave the notario publico was all we had."

What Rodrigo didn't know is that notraio publico's in the USA were not the same as those found in Mexico. In the USA, they were just a notary public. This meant they were credentialed to certify the signing of documents. In no way were they qualified or allowed to give legal advice or even assist in filling out forms. This didn't stop them from exploiting a desperate community that needed significantly more services.[xxiii]

"I am so sorry. I'm counting on my Aunt Rosa to hire a legit lawyer to represent me. Maybe he can find someone who would work pro bono for you." said Miguel.

CHAPTER NINETEEN

Alex made sure her bedroom door was locked and sat down in front of her computer. She wasn't allowed to tell her parents that she wasn't a barely-employed, struggling race walker. After graduating, Homeland Security recruited her as a white hat to investigate cybercrimes. Drexel had a great reputation for graduating students ready to contribute to the workforce. Adding her exploits with Media Titan she had the computing credentials needed to impress recruiters with the highest standards. Given her affinity for travel and perfect cover as a race walker, she could fly almost anywhere without being suspicious. As a young millennial and gamer, she could fit in perfect with the dark web crowd. While some might recognize her from the Media Titan fiasco, it only added to her street cred.

Sure, she had access to all sorts of advanced cyber security tools at her disposal, but when you have the ability to drop a keylogger directly on a suspect's computer all sorts of doors open. Poor Pedro would have no idea he was being watched.

"Let's see what's up," thought Alex as she restored her computer from Hibernate mode. Oddly Microsoft disabled Hibernate mode by default in Windows 10. Alex always tried to save as much energy as possible and therefore didn't want to waste energy leaving a computer in Sleep mode which still used a modicum of energy. She didn't want to completely shut the computer off, because that would have required reopening all her programs. Alex turned the option back on so she could save her current status to the hard drive and completely power down. It took a few extra seconds to boot back, but it was a tradeoff she was willing to make. Sadly, when she used her gaming rig at home it sucked so much power up while in use the savings was more in spirit than a significant portion of her energy usage.

When the screen popped on, her many browsers opened and refreshed to the latest copies of their contents. Fox News was living up to its reputation with headlines like:

`"The New Deplorables? Obamas guilty of unethical behavior…"` and `"Love is a Battlefield, DC consultant accuses wife of revenge plot over claims of affair with Omar."`

"Two of their favorite targets," thought Alex. It always amazed her just how obvious their obsessions were.

MSNBC had a bit of a broader approach with stories including on the UK political chaos, the gun control controversy, and former Defense Secretary Mattis's interviews from the morning.

Sadly, the only area of overlap was the coverage of Hurricane Dorian. *"Yeah, the one where Trump played golf while people were boarding up their houses. Does he not get the hypocrisy given that he was so critical of Obama's time spent golfing?"* thought Alex.[xxiv]

Thinking she shouldn't waste time; she couldn't resist checking out www.trumpgolfcount.com.

`Trump Golf Count: 213*`

`Cost to Taxpayers: About $109,000,000**`

`*Daytime visits to golf clubs since inauguration, with evidence of playing golf on at least 98 visits. Our last recorded outing was on September 2, 2019. Click on complete data table for a list of Trump's outings, or view our breakdown of total costs.`

Read about the new GAO report on the cost of Trump's trips to Mar-a-Lago.

"That's crazy," thought Alex. The total was more than two and a half times more than the pace Obama played golf.[xxv] Trump must have been suffering from temporary amnesia as he was quoted over twenty times criticizing Obama's golf habits.[xxvi]

"Oh well, enough of a distraction," she flipped to another virtual desktop hiding all of her current windows and bringing up her work view.

She securely connected to Homeland Security's VPN and starting the endless task that's the bane of every modern employee, sifting through the countless emails that came in since she last logged on.

As she was, a calendar reminder popped up:

"Status report due: Vinnie"

Vinnie was also her boss and his management style worked great for Alex who liked a less rigid structure. He understood keeping Alex on a long leash to let her follow her hunches. Still there was accountability and she needed to report back regularly with her progress.

Alex's efforts in Mexico had paid off dramatically. After placing a virus that was both a keystroke logger and transmitted his webcam/mic on Pedro's computer she was able to see everything that he typed and if necessary, watch what was going on in his room. She had access to every online account he interacted with since the night they met. She also noticed he spent an uncomfortable amount of time looking at the photos/videos of her. She thought, *"God, I don't want to turn the webcam on while he's looking at them. I might be permanently damaged."*

Pedro's company, DataRex, was based in the United States. Once the king of ubiquitous and universally aggravating popup ads, their business had declined for years. Aggressive efforts by companies like Google recognized that improving the Internet browsing experience of its Chrome users was paramount to their own ad network. Google's "do no harm" philosophy was not necessarily more altruistic than anyone else, it's always about following the money.

DataRex grew a huge business within completely legal, but dubious, moral ground. It wasn't enough to sell pop-ups on websites that were either advertising their own goods and services or getting revenue from the ads hosted from the site itself. Instead, through numerous creative methods, they hijacked the browser itself and propagated unfiltered ads so that all the revenue went into DataRex's coffers.

Their preferred method of choice was to piggyback their software with valuable open source software or as an extension to Chrome. They might even create software that was valuable to the masses of ignorant users and then sandwich their software in the installation. All of this was disclosed on page 100 of the terms and conditions that nearly everyone accepts without thought.

While Google intelligently blocked all extensions not approved for the Chrome store, DataRex was smarter. They outsourced breaking Chrome and discovered a loophole; enterprise plug-ins were still allowed. A little trickery later, and they were back in business for a while.

When that avenue was closed, they resorted to slickly written spam emails. The latest unsolicited emails even had buttons to report the email as spam. However, what the button really did was report back to DataRex that the email account was valid and ripe for additional spam emails.

The savvy CEO Jeremiah Lechtenberg was always two steps ahead of the game. The big money was no longer in ads, now it was in herding public opinion. Initially client requests were as innocuous as helping them improve corporate reputations when unflattering reviews were posted.

That's where employees like Pedro came in. There were countless clients willing to pay for unique reviews written for their projects. Sure, computer automation could produce reasonable reviews, but companies were improving their detection methods just as fast as DataRex was rolling out new schemes. A better approach was inexpensive labor like Pedro who had a relatively strong command of English. Poor grammar is an easy way to tell when a review is fake, even though many native Americans struggled to write complete sentences. His skills made him an excellent candidate for his position and he quickly developed favor with his bosses for his excellent work.

While there was money to be made with false reviews, by the time the 2016 elections rolled around DataRex evolved into a silent leader in generating a combination of fake news to prompt public opinion or true posts with controversial opinions to get people in the USA fighting with each other. Posts to either Facebook, Instagram or Twitter were filled with racial tones from "Black Man You've Been Sleep for Far Too Long," to "Unite the Right."

There were equal calls to stir the religious pot. An image depicting Jesus with the phrase "Like if you believe, Keep scrolling if you don't," was liked more than any other in 2016 before the election. No pop culture icon was safe from exploitation. Whether it was Miss Piggy stirring the battle of the sexes or Homer Simpson provoking the mistreatment of people by the police, the hidden purpose was the same, to fuel discontent between Americans.[xxvii]

The darker side of the business grew rapidly by assisting with the propagation of false product / service reviews. Figuring out where DataRex drew the line was the focus of Alex's current case.

Once she had a view of everything he typed, she didn't just monitor what he did, but focused on infecting as many of his coworkers' computers as well. The latest count was 17 infected computers, and a total of 58 accounts that she gathered passwords from. "Not bad for a few day's work," Alex applauded herself.

She sent the statistics off to Vinnie knowing she would call in later in that day to provide a more descriptive accounting of her activities.

CHAPTER TWENTY

Mark Belcastro let out a sigh, as he walked into the York Correctional facility. He had been through the mundane routine too many times, but liked to get an early start to his day and get the tedium over with. His visits started at 7:00 AM, well before the hustle and bustle caused when formal visitation hours begin.

"Good morning Mark," the guard greeting him like an old friend.

"Morning," Mark answered as he formally showed his ID, pulled out his keys, cellphone and coins and placed them in a tray. He then passed his briefcase through the x-ray machine and walked through the metal detector. He wondered what this case would unveil. On paper, Miguel looked harmless, but how often was he deceived by first appearances?

Miguel woke to a rough shove in his barracks, "Lawyer's here, Vamanos."

"What are they waking me for? Wait, I have a lawyer?" asked Miguel to himself. Even though Miguel was used to getting up early, he reluctantly arose. Since entering the detention sleep was the only place he could find peace. He quickly got to his feet as he had witnessed more than one inmate abused by the guards for their tardiness when called to a task. He followed the guard to the visitation room.

Mark extended his hand, "Hi Miguel, I am Mark Belcastro. Last night your aunt hired me to represent you."

Miguel shook his hand and sat down at the plastic table. "Where's my aunt?" inquired Miguel.

Mark opened his briefcase, "She would like to be here, but these visitations are for legal counsel only. So, let's get down to business. Listen Miguel, your deportation officer is going to press you to take a deal for voluntary departure. Do not under any circumstances sign anything without me present."

"Are they going to send me back to Mexico sir?" asked Miguel.

"Right now, we have to focus on getting you out on bond, we will worry about your permanent status later. OK?" Mark said. He was very particular about the order he accomplished each task. Perhaps he had inherited a little more Obsessive Compulsive Disorder (OCD) from his father than he cared to admit. He always justified his behavior as using OCD for the power of good, since it kept him organized. He never heard the echoes of the same justifications his father used to use when his mother would complain to him about his rigidness. Mark also knew he had to keep the pace moving. He didn't want to get bogged down in anything other than the matter at hand. Making a profit meant moving through as many cases as quickly as he could.

"What we need to do," Mark continued without pause, "is to show why the judge should set a reasonable bond for your release. I need you to give me as much information about your life here since you entered the United States."

Miguel cleared his throat, "Well, after I arrived, I took any job I could get. First, I worked at a local gas station. Then after a few months, I got a job cleaning dishes at the local pub. It was there that I met Julia's mother. She was a waitress working her way through college," Miguel smiled and paused.

"We were in love. I was in heaven, but she got pregnant and couldn't deal with a child in her life. She wanted to focus on her degree. She agreed to have the baby only if I assumed full responsibility. Of course, I did because what greater gift is there in life, right? But it meant losing her mother. Just after she was born, I got a job with Uber and I have been with them for several years. I even have a five-star rating. I saved enough to get Julia some new clothes and the backpack she wanted for school that she started this year," Miguel lost his voice for a moment.

"She must be so scared, you have to get me back to her, please."

Mark nodded, "That's the idea, please tell me more about your family here."

Miguel squeezed his eyes shut and pictured his daughter. Her long, black flowing hair framed a devilish, inviting smile that could melt the coldest of hearts. When Julia went through the neighborhood on Halloween, her bag filled faster than most. She charmed all who she encountered. Parents would often give her more pieces of candy just to see her smile beam even brighter.

"Well my daughter and I live with my aunt. We go to church every Sunday. We also love to go to the park in our free time. She brings bread for the pigeons and I bring a chicken torta to a homeless woman who is always there looking sad. It makes her smile to have a taste of home," explained Miguel.

"I checked and you have a no criminal record and no driving violations. Is there anything negative about you or your circumstance that might come up about you?"

"No, sir. I've been a clean as can be. Not even a parking ticket," Miguel said with the first bit of positivity since he got arrested.

Mark raised an eyebrow, "Does that include things like drinking and gambling."

Now Miguel laughed, "Sir, I don't have money for either one, but I am not interested in those things."

Mark nodded and made notes, he continued, "Have you ever been diagnosed with a mental illness?"

Miguel shook his head no.

"Have you been in any physical fights since you arrived or angered anyone?"

Miguel cleared his throat, "I may annoy Aunt Rosa from time to time, but my goal since I arrived was to keep a low profile and be a ghost."

"Is there anything else you can tell me to help build your case," Mark asked?

Thinking hard for something more Miguel said, "Well I don't think this counts for much, but I always pick up trash on the ground when I see it. People in this country take for granted how blessed they are to live in such a wonderful place. It drives me crazy that people are so thoughtless, and I want to be a good example for my daughter. Really that drives everything that I do. Even when she is not with me, I ask myself, would I want her to copy what I am doing? If I don't like the answer, I don't do it."

Finally, Mark nodded with an approving smile, "Now that I can use. And that low-profile goal, keep that up because in here you really do want to be a ghost."

Mark passed some papers to Miguel, "Now I want you to read these. They explain the process in which we will apply to keep you in the United States. It includes Form I-589, which we will use to apply for asylum. Be prepared to give me all of the information on the form after I get you out at the bond determination hearing."

Miquel was actually familiar with applying for asylum this way. It's something many undocumented immigrants talked about. "But, sir, I entered the United States well over a year ago. I thought I couldn't apply for asylum this way."

"Miguel, that's why you have me. We'll explain to the judge that circumstances have changed in Mexico and that's why you can't return," explained Mark.

Miguel was about to protest, but decided he needed to be respectful. Miguel hesitated before making a request, "If you speak to my aunt, please ask her to tell Julia that daddy will be home as soon as he can and that I love them both."

Mark shook his hand, "Will do. Last night, when she hired me, I also explained the visitation procedures. With any luck, we'll quickly get your hearing and you won't have to worry about it."

Miguel blinked back tears of gratitude and smiled at Mark.

Miguel had a singular goal for the rest of the day. He was going to read through the paperwork carefully and make sure he was ready to provide any answers necessary when Mark returned.

He did take a break to ask the guard how he would find out if his aunt was scheduled to visit, but was scoffed at by the guard who growled, "Not now, I am busy."

His particular form of busy was swiping back and forth on Tinder selecting girls he wanted to date. *"Who would date such an ass?"* wondered Miguel.

Defeated for now, Miguel refocused his attention to the legal papers in front of him. Miguel struggled to read accurately in English. He settled in and dove into the material.

Shortly after what the detention center called dinner, Miguel drifted off to a heavy sleep from all the stress of the day. He woke in the middle of the night to an inmate that didn't belong in his cell block standing over his bed. At once awake and electrified. Miguel, hissed, "Step off man."

His visitor chuckled, "I'll see you soon Miggie."

Miguel did not sleep after that, he heard stories of what happened in places like these but had been left alone so far. He wanted to keep it that way, he just didn't know how. "So much for finding release in sleep," Miguel thought as he stared at the barren walls.

CHAPTER TWENTY-ONE

Alex arose early to get her race walk in before most of the town woke up. While visiting her dad was always stressful, she relished walking in the heavily wooded streets of Medford. She particularly enjoyed weaving in and out of the streets that were littered with tiny private lakes and quaint, welcoming log cabins. While it could look like a summer town, most Medford locals were permanent residents.

An added bonus for her aging body was that the streets weren't heavily traveled with traffic. This allowed to walk down the middle of the street, which was preferred because walking on the top of the road's crown was the least abusive part of the road to her body.

As she pulled onto her block, she slowed from a race walk to a pedestrian gait. It was then that one of her dad's best friends in the neighborhood popped out to pick up his morning paper. *"Do people still read those things,"* thought Alex.

"Good morning Mr. Grimes." Growing up, Alex always liked Mr. Grimes but as political polarization grew, it became harder and harder to respect him. People can certainly disagree on matters of opinion; morality is certainly subjective. However, it was Mr. Grimes inability to agree on the facts that really frustrated her. It didn't help matters that he was the first to pop out political signs in his yard. It wasn't just one either. He had numerous signs for each major race of an election.

"Welcome home, Alex. I see you are still at that speed walking thing."

"Um, that's race walking Mr. Grimes." Alex pondered how after all these years he couldn't get that right. It was just one of the many "facts" that Mr. Grimes twisted. This was one fact she had corrected him on countless occasions, yet he'd call it "power walking", "fitness walking", or "doing that heel-toe thing."

"Your dad tells me that's all you do. Can you really support yourself that way?" asked Mr. Grimes.

"I get by. I give a lot of lessons to older people who are out of shape," Alex said wondering if he would get the slight dig at his "Retirement belly" as he jokingly called it.

"With this being 'the greatest Economy in the History of America' you certainly can find a job with that expensive degree of yours." Mr. Grimes baited her.

"Did he want a fight?" she wondered. Alex was never one to pass up a political argument. She obviously couldn't tell him what she was secretly working for Homeland Security's Cybercrimes Division, but was more than happy to correct his parroting of President Trump's dubious claims of the economy. "How's that Mr. Grimes?"

"We have the lowest unemployment in nearly fifty years!" Mr. Grimes explained.

"Well, yes you can thank President Obama for that. He inherited arguably the worst economic mess since the Great Depression and turned it around into a job growing machine. If you look at the numbers, numbers I might point out Candidate Trump said were fake and made up, the number of jobs created per month for the first few years of President Trump's term were almost identical from when Obama turned it around. Lately, that's not even true, with fewer and fewer jobs being created recently," Alex fired back.[xxviii]

"Well GDP under Obama was horrible. What recovery averages under three percent?"

"Um, well Trump's economic miracle hasn't averaged that either and it's been over a year since that historic tax cut was supposed to not only jumpstart the economy, but pay for itself. Neither of those things have happened."

Before Mr. Grimes could reply Alex added, "Mr. Grimes, respectfully, aren't you a deficit hawk? Weren't you complaining during the Obama administration that half a billion-dollar deficit is too high and didn't Trump say he would eliminate the national debt in eight years?"

"Well there are bigger problems, like your party's socialist agenda led by AOC and the squad!" Mr. Grimes said trying ineffectively to defend an indefensible position.

"That's a pretty interesting stance to take from someone who made their salary as a public high school teacher and is currently living off Social Security, Medicare, and a public pension. That sounds like a pretty socialist existence if you ask me." Alex had prepared that one in advance.

"Did you learn to be disrespectful at the liberal college of yours Alex? I paid in exactly what I was supposed to for my pension, so it's fully funded."

Alex had heard Mr. Grimes make this claim to her father before, and therefore did the math herself. Mr. Grimes explanation seemed too good to be true. "Have you ever done the math Mr. Grimes?"

"Well I don't have time for such things, I am a very busy man," defended Mr. Grimes.

"Perhaps if you spent less time watching Fox News, you might understand that the underfunding of your pension is just part of the near $6 trillion dollar unfunded liability."[xxix]

In the final defensive of most right-wing zealots he barked, "That's more fake news!" Mr. Grimes concluded.

"On that note Mr. Grimes, I think I should leave you to read your paper." Alex continued her cooldown now needing to both cooldown from walking and talking.

CHAPTER TWENTY-TWO

Vinny set up multiple applications for FISA warrants for the suspected leaders of The Collective. As was typical of the application process, all were accepted. During the entire existence of the FISA court over 30,000 warrants were submitted at an alarming 99.97% acceptance rate leading many to believe the court was a rubber stamp for surveillance.[xxx]

Once the warrant was received, Vinnie had agents follow the top suspects of The Collective with a van equipped with a highly controversial device commonly known as a stingray. The device acted like a cell tower. Since phones locked onto the strongest local signal, the stingray would be set to a very powerful signal strength, making it the default choice of all cell phones within range. The stingray acted as if it were the carrier for the phones it misdirected. People making calls, texts or surfing the Internet would have no idea that their unencrypted information could be snooped. A stingray also allowed the government to locate a person's phone while it was on and not in airplane mode with extreme accuracy.

There were many privacy concerns using a stingray device. Often, law enforcement used the devices without a proper warrant. When they did get an official warrant, the device captured data for many more phones than just the targeted phone.

The use of a stingray device wasn't a perfect solution. The target had to be in proximity of the device in order for it to have a strong enough signal to overpower the nearby cell towers and did not provide access to encrypted traffic.

The data Vinny's team was able to gather was a combination of location, unencrypted calls and texts, and a large amount of encrypted traffic. Often, people looking to hide correspondence from the peering eyes of the government use programs like the Signal app to encrypt data on both sides of the conversation. While Signal worked well, it did require both parties to install and use the app. So, it worked well for the semi-sophisticated crowd, but if a user had to make a call or text to a non-Signal user it left them wide open to be snooped.

The data gathered in the field was sent to Homeland Security's servers where Traya was gathering and correlating as much data as he could.

CHAPTER TWENTY-THREE

Miguel sat in a holding cell, patiently waiting for the judge to call his name. There was no fancy suit for him to wear like he saw on many legal TV shows. Instead, he was wearing federally issued orange jumpsuits that screamed criminal. The suit had York Detention Center printed on the back and didn't fit particularly well.

The room was sparsely decorated, except for a small analog clock on the wall. Miguel watched the second hand tick off, one second at a time. "Could it move any slower?" thought Miguel to himself.

He watched one by one as people were called into the courtroom before him. Miguel had no way of knowing how long he would have to wait. Not knowing anything that was going on in the courtroom was equally maddening.

Finally, it was time in the courtroom for Miguel's case. Judge Gaudet was dressed in traditional black robes. In his upper fifties, he had spent way too much of his life sitting in court and while the robes hid his obesity, his puffy face did not. "Case A:205-123-856, Lopez, Miguel. Will counsel for Mr. Lopez please come to the counsel table and be seated," Judge Gaudet called out. Mark Belcastro followed the judge's instructions as a guard went to retrieve Miguel.

Miguel walked with the guard into the courtroom. Miguel's eyes darted around the room until he saw his aunt and minister sitting on the far side. When his aunt looked over, he tried to give her a reassuring smile that he was ok.

The reality was far different. His hands were visibly shaking. Miguel hadn't been this nervous since he found out Julia's mom was pregnant. While it seemed like Judge Gaudet was a reasonable man and according to his lawyer was as known to give people as fair of a shake as anyone would, he couldn't help but feel the pending doom of deportation creeping in on himself.

Miguel sheepishly walked up beside his lawyer. "Here, Your Honor," Miguel stated as respectfully as he could muster and then as he was coached by his lawyer he sat down beside Mark.

In a rather monotone voice, Judge Gaudet continued, "Mr. Lopez is alleged to the following. One, Mr. Lopez is not a citizen of the United States. Two, he is a national of Mexico. Three, he entered the United States without presenting himself at the border."

Miguel felt uncomfortable as the list of allegations against him were stated. *"Was it really such a crime to want to feel safe?"* Miguel thought to himself.

Then the judge and asked Miguel, "Do you wish Mark Belcastro to represent you in these matters?"

"Do I have any better options," Miguel thought to himself, but merely replied, "Yes, Your Honor."

The judge moved on, "Mr. Belcastro, do you deny the allegations against Mr. Lopez?"

Mark conceded, "You are correct Your Honor. We are not disputing the facts."

The judge continued, "According to your written request for a release on bond, you entered the country as a minor, at the age of 16 and in 2008. As I am sure you are aware, that makes you ineligible for protection under DACA."

Miguel understood this, as all illegal immigrants knew the importance of certain dates and ages in determining their ability to request to remain in the United States. In order to be eligible for DACA protection a Miguel would have had to have arrived before June 2007 and younger than 16.

"However, I do see that you have no criminal record since coming to the United States and you have a daughter," continued Judge Gaudet.

Belcastro cleared his throat and looked down at Miguel, giving him a much-needed smile. "Your Honor, Miguel does indeed have a young five-year old daughter whom he has sole custody of. She also has a United States birth certificate. If it pleases the court, I'd like to introduce ..."

Judge Gaudet interrupted immediately, "Mr. Belcastro you know better than that. You are supposed to supply all such documentation to the court ahead of time."

"I am sorry Your Honor. May I submit it now?" Belcastro waited for approval from the judge and handed it to the bailiff.

Gaudet skimmed the certificate and redirected his attention to Belcastro and Miguel, "If Mr. Lopez is released on bond, where will Mr. Lopez be residing?"

"Your Honor, Mr. Lopez was residing with his aunt and daughter and will, with your permission, continue to reside with them." Belcastro had done this dance with many judges before. He was used to painting a rosy picture of his client's lives. Belcastro also volunteered, "Mr. Lopez also has strong ties to the community. He attends church regularly and volunteers at the church on a regular basis."

The judge seemingly ignored Belcastro's attempt to sugarcoat Miguel's situation and inquired, "And what is the legal status of this aunt?"

"She is a lawful permanent resident, Your Honor," replied Belcastro.

Seemingly satisfied with the answers provided, the judge asked, "What type of application is Mr. Lopez applying for?"

"Your Honor, Mr. Lopez is applying for asylum," responded Belcastro.

"Of course, he is," thought Judge Gaudet. He then looked over his paperwork. "So, I see you are an Uber driver with no traffic violations. That's excellent."

"Your Honor, if I my interject," the lawyer for DHS politely interrupted.

"What do you have to say Ms. Burnett?" the judge asked.

"I would like to point out that while Mr. Lopez illegally resides in Wallingford, PA, he is in possession of a Maryland license plate. One has to assume he obtained that license through fraudulently representing his home address," Ms. Burnett stated.

Belcastro then came to Miguel's defense, "Your Honor, that may be true, but it was to provide for his family."

The judged replied, "Gentlemen, we've all seen this situation before, I'll take it under advisement. How many hours a week does Mr. Lopez work?"

"It fluctuates depending on his aunt's schedule, but he tries to work at least 40 hours a week. I would like to enter into evidence his last two months work records that show a consistent pattern of responsible work ethic and five-star reviews," responded Belcastro.

"Mr. Belcastro, I assume you have documents endorsing Mr. Lopez's character a community standing."

"Yes, of course Your Honor. We have brought five letters, including one from his aunt, his minister, and three friends. In fact, his aunt and Minister Sheppard are sitting in the corner."

The judge pondered the facts in front of him. They were no different than many of the cases presented daily. While the news highlights the atrocities that involve some of illegal immigrants, the truth is criminal rates amongst illegal immigrants are often lower than the general population.[xxxi]

Then the judge made his ruling, "Mr. Lopez, you certainly do not appear to be a flight risk. Given your lack of criminal record, strong family, and community ties, as well as your employment record, I am setting the bond at $5,000."

Belcastro whispers to Miguel, "I told your aunt to have the funds available. If she does, she can get a bank check written today and you can be out by this afternoon."

Miguel felt unbelievable pains of remorse. He knew his aunt's finances and couldn't imagine where she would get that much money from. After moving to the new house, all of the additional unexpected expenses ate up the remaining disposable cash she had. He had about $2,000 saved in an account that he had his aunt cosign on just in case she had to take care of Julia but wondered where the rest came from.

Miguel whispered back, "Thank you, sir!" The reality of being home with his daughter began to diminish his feelings of guilt.

"If you are released, you can come by my office tomorrow and we can start preparing your case. Just be aware if you do not return when requested, your aunt will lose the entirety of her bond."

"I understand," replied Miguel. Then, on cue from Belcastro, Miguel also thanked the judge and they left the courtroom.[xxxii]

CHAPTER TWENTY-FOUR

Alex sat back down in front of her computer. It was time to do the real work and expand the reach of her data collection. With a list of email addresses, social media contacts, and passwords, Alex's grasp was enormous.

The first and easiest attempt was to check email addresses on www.haveibeenpwned.com. The website is setup to inform people if their email addresses were found in breeched data from websites they may have created accounts on. A user, upon finding out that their email address is listed on a breached site, should change their passwords for that account and any other accounts associated with that email address.

Sometimes the information gathered from breaches was harmless, but other times it might include hacks of the actual password. While the website didn't make the hacked data available to the public, Alex had access to the hacked data from the Homeland Security data repositories and could look up pertinent information as needed. If the data was robust enough, she could use it directly. Otherwise it helped inform other attacks she used to breach a target's accounts.

Everyone by now is familiar with the phishing scams where they were told they could receive millions of dollars if you just reached back out to them.

Of course, there was no pot of gold at the end of the email chain. The phishers were trying to gain either personal information they could sell on the black market or to trick you into sending money. People's stupidity and greed should never be underestimated.

Given the data Alex had, she engaged in a far more effective spear phishing campaign. Spear phishing used personal information about the target to make the scam more believable. In this case, the scam wasn't to steal money, but information.

Her goal today was to hack into three more accounts. First up, Juan Martìnez. He was a friend of Pedro's at work and was connected to Pedro on Facebook. From the number of social media posts, it also appeared, they were drinking buddies.

Scanning Juan's friend list there was a disturbingly large number of high school aged girls he was friends with. *"Time for the sextortion scam,"* thought Alex.

Alex opens one of hundreds of email accounts she has set up for this kind of work and sends an email from InternetWatcher07@gmail.com.

```
I know what you've been doing with all those
young girls. You should have covered your
webcam if you were going to please yourself
while watching them. Don't worry, I'm not law
enforcement. If you do as I say, we won't
publish the videos we have of you onto social
media. That's right imagine videos of you
touching yourself on Facebook, Twitter,
Instagram and other websites. Your family will
disown you. Your friends will mock you, and
you'll probably get fired from your job at
DataRex.

Don't believe me? I've included a short clip of
you in this email. Watch it and then send us
$100 in bitcoin and we'll destroy our copy of
the video.

Regards

Internet Watcher
```

By name dropping DataRex it added an authenticity to the email that would make Juan afraid to not believe its validity. Alex didn't really want the money and the video sent wasn't an actual video. Instead it was more malware designed to track his computer activities.

The goal wasn't to catch or extort the small fish that she caught so far, but to work her way up to the managers where she could get intel on the sources of their work.

She cast another line. This time Sofia Sanchez from Mexico City was her target. She also worked with Pedro. Sofia was an attractive young woman with a bit of the millennial disease resulting in the "need" to over post. Photos of her with different outfits and accessories littered her wall.

From SocialMediaInfluencerPromo@SocialMediaInfluencersPromotion.com.

Dear Sofia,

We are very impressed with your stylistic flair. Your sense of posing in your photos as well as your accessorizing is wonderful. I work for a company that gives social media influencers, like yourself, free products in exchange for product placement in your social media feeds. Each month, we have a wide selection of products that you can select from for which we would ask you to post images of yourself using them to Instagram, Twitter and Facebook. You may select up to three products a month and they will be delivered to your residence free of charge. We will review your success every quarter and if pleased with the results of your engagement we will renew this agreement for another three months. To get started, please sign the enclosed agreement and log into the website www.SocialMediaInfluencersPromotion.com to download our private application. You can log in with the credentials SofiaSanchez and the temporary password A34CuG!$Z>10. We look forward to working with you.

Sincerely

Juana Perez

Social Media Promotions, Inc.

Alex looked over a few more social media accounts of the people who were friends of Pedro from DataRex. She settled in on attempting to spear fish Antonio Hernández, a middle-aged deportee who had two daughters in public schools. Alex looked over down at her watch. "Timing is perfect," she thought.

She felt bad using the atomic bomb of spear phishing and wrote the following.

Antonio

We have your daughter Gabriella. She is quite cute with her ponytails and innocent smile. If you ever want to see her again, you must do exactly what we tell you. We are already monitoring your phones, email and social media accounts. Any attempt to contact the police or for that matter anyone will result in your daughter's death.

Reply that you understand.

Alex added the description from a photo of Antonio's daughter he posted to Instagram the night before. She didn't sign it or make a request on purpose. Studies showed that it was more effective to heighten a person's paranoia and leave them hanging than it was to make the ask right away.

CHAPTER TWENTY-FIVE

As Miguel was about to be released, the guard sneered at him. Miguel's phone was sitting out on the counter in front of Miguel, but as he went to reach for it the guard pulled it back. He looked at Miguel with disgust, "You know we got three types of people here in America. Good people who belong here, average people who belong here, and bad people who belong here. What don't belong are the cockroaches," he shoved the phone at Miguel.

Miguel knew better than to react to the guard's taunts. What he wanted to say was "better to be an unwanted cockroach than dead." He could still see the severed head swinging in hands of the monster back in Mexico. Instead, he simply took the phone and said, "Thank you sir."

The guard unlocked the series of doors and gates and gave Miguel a final, unceremonious shove out the final gate and back into society.

Miguel looked up at the sky, took a deep breath of fresh air and thanked Jesus that he was still in the States at least for now. Since his aunt was working and Julia was at school, Miguel had no way to get home. He had no money, but he had his phone. In a bit of irony, he called Uber.

After a few short minutes, a blue Honda Accord approached as was indicated by the app. Miguel knew his driver Juan was here and he was one step closer to home. Miguel hated to admit it, but when the app popped up Juan's name and photo avatar, he was grateful to see someone who was Hispanic. The disrespect and disgust from the detention center was scarring. He just didn't have the strength right now to deal with more hatred.

Miguel smiled hesitantly as he entered the car, "Thank you for accepting the ride."

He smiled, "Hermano, anytime my friend. I have unfortunately picked up too many of our amigos from here over the past two years. I understand too well how things work for us around here these days. Presumed guilty and deported unless proven innocent."

Miguel was grateful to have an empathetic driver for his ride. Right now, he couldn't wait to be home, and even more couldn't wait for his daughter to come from school so he could hug her. A feeble, "Gracias amigo," was all Miguel could muster.

Juan took a good look at Miguel in the rear view mirror. He imagined that Miguel was much like himself, a good man, a family man who stood to lose everything. Juan lost his brother to ICE only one year ago and now he was in the United States alone. Ever since then he drove extra hours so he could send money home to his brother who was still struggling to find a legal job.

The trip should have been a little over an hour and a half, but after turning onto the *parking lot* of the Blue Route (as I-476 is referred to), traffic ground to a halt. Miguel had experienced the frustration of many of his clients when faced with interminable delays. The juxtaposition was not a comfortable one.

Juan could see Miguel's frustration building, "Don't worry amigo, we'll be there soon."

"I know. I am an Uber driver as well. I've suffered along this route many times. I am just anxious to get home to my family." Miguel rarely had to take an Uber himself and always thought they should get discounts, but Uber's razor thin margins and consistent losses negated that possibility.

As they arrived at Miguel's house Juan took Miguel's hand, "No tip, please don't argue, save it for your family. I will pray for you."

Brought to the brink of tears Miguel, squeezed Juan's hand. It was amazing to feel acceptance and support when it is so scarce. Miguel shook his hand vigorously, "Muchas gracias,"

Juan smiled, "De nada; Just be there for your family."

That was exactly what Miguel intended to do. He fished for the spare key hidden behind a series of planters they had on the back steps.

Miguel entered his home and looked at the walls littered with photos of Julia. All the photos had one thing in common: Julia's beaming smile. No matter what the setting, Julia always wore a bright, big smile on her face. It was like she was singing I love life without moving her lips. He hoped that his current predicament wouldn't take that smile away. Miguel knew he needed to talk to her about their new reality, but how to do that was still a mystery.

Miguel arrived way too early to the bus stop. He didn't want to miss a minute of the time he'd have with Julia because it could end at any moment. He watched the earlier buses stop, let off kids and continue along its route. Waiting seemed endless as he peered down the block, happy and anxious simultaneously. He wondered what Julia's mother would think if she knew what was happening in his life. Should he contact her? Could he contact her? His shoulders softened a little as he remembered the feel of her embrace. She never even held her daughter. They could have been a family, but she chose her career. He shook himself back to the present as the school bus slowed to a stop.

Miguel saw Julia in her usual seat in the back of the bus. She was daydreaming out the window with a solemn stare. *"Did I steal my angel's smile?"* wondered Miguel.

Then as the bus slowed to a stop, Julia's gaze looked up and she caught a glimpse of Miguel through the window. Julia's smile broadened and seemingly lit up the bus. She immediately ran off the bus with her backpack bobbing up and down.

"Papa!" she screamed and ran with outstretched arms to embrace her father. "I missed you this much," she stretched her arms out wide.

"And I missed you this much more," Miguel stretched his arms as wide as he could. Then Julia leaped into his arms.

"Auntie said you were away for a special job, but I know we're more special than any job, right?" Her brown eyes looked up at Miguel with eager anticipation.

"You are the most special thing in my life. You know that!"

Miguel took her tiny hand in his as they entered the house. *"Am I ready for this?"* he asked himself. *"Yes, be strong,"* he replied in his head.

"Remember the morning you woke up and daddy was not there? Well, that is because I was taken away by some official people who work for the government."

Julia's smile faded, "Why would they take you Daddy? You didn't do anything wrong."

Seeing Julia go dim broke his heart. After a long hug, Miguel built up his courage again, "Julia, I need you to come and sit with me. We always say honesty is numero uno so there is something I need to tell you."

Julia sensed the seriousness of the moment and dropped her backpack to sit next to her father. "OK Papa, I listen."

Miguel drew a long breath, "Julia you know I try to be a good role model, but daddy did make a mistake before you were born. A long time ago your nana sent me here to be safe. I came into the country without the right paperwork and that means that I entered the USA illegally."

Julia looked confused, "Does that make you a criminal Papa?"

Miguel didn't quite know how to answer that. "Well, I think that depends who you ask. Now that the government knows about it, they will decide if I can stay or if I have to leave."

Julia was scared but knew she had to be brave, "Okay, well, of course, they will let you stay. You are a great dad and I need you."

"If only it were that simple," Miguel wanted to scream, instead he said, "I hope that is true mi conejita, but if it isn't there is a chance I will have to go back to Mexico. I need you to promise me something. I need you to promise that you will be okay and continue to be the beautiful girl that you are."

Julia shook her head vigorously, "No! If you go, then I go."

"It's not that simple honey, there are many reasons that you cannot go to Mexico."

She crossed her arms and looked up with determination. She was so much like her mother it gave him chills. With her chin held high she questioned Miguel, "Why can't I go if you have to go?"

Miguel began to imagine the horrible ways in which MS-13 could punish him by torturing Julia. They could easily pick her up from school and she would be terrified. He could hear her trembling voice on the phone, "Daddy, they haven't hurt me yet, but they say they will unless you do what they ask." He would have no choice but to work for them to keep her safe.

Julia's voice broke through his frightening daydream, "It's that bad in Mexico, Daddy?"

Miguel shuddered, "Yes, Julia it is that bad. That is why I came here the way I did. If I stayed, I would have been forced to do terrible things to people. If you were to go back with me, they would threaten to do bad things to you if I don't do bad things for them."

Julia considered this new reality and thrust her chin higher, "Okay, well if I can't go to Mexico, then you can't go either."

Miguel let out an anxious sigh, "That is the plan. Then with any luck, Daddy will stay right where he is." He put his arm around his daughter and sank into the couch.

CHAPTER TWENTY-SIX

Alex monitored her three new targets as well as the accounts of others. Her screen looked like a stockbroker's dashboard. Alex knew better than to have Facebook open in window while she was working, but when a post came up on a respected race walking coach claiming there was no climate crisis she couldn't resist starting a battle of words.

Coach Ken: I completely recognize that climate change is real, but we are not in a crisis.

Alex: If you believe the scientists that we have climate change, why do you not believe them when they say it's a crisis? I've traveled to six continents and have seen the dramatic change in glaciers firsthand. That was long before years of record heat. No glaciers = no water = no food = no people. Ahhh no crisis, let's get rid of all the people ;)

A person who wasn't a "friend" responded as well.

SmartyPants: Alex, if the glaciers melted wouldn't that mean more water? 😕

Alex: SmartyPants, please study science. Only temporarily and yes before you say it, at one-point scientists thought we could go to another ice age. Scientists are not always right. When presented with more evidence they can change their opinion. Diet has changed with more evidence. Do you want to go back to the science of the 70s for your health?

Then Coach Ken replied, infographic at the ready.

Coach Ken: Because we've been here before.

Ken's posts a graph showing the many warming and cooling periods of the earth.

GLOBAL TEMPERATURES
(2500 BC TO 2007 AD

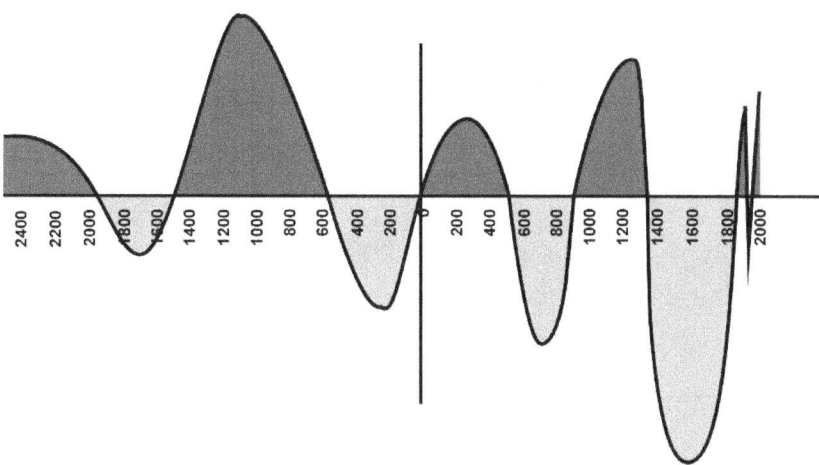

Alex: Coach Ken, you are making the scientist's point. The evidence of what's different is right there. Look at the current slope of warming. It's much steeper. Just as extinctions will always happen, it's a question of how many and over what period of time. Given the current rate of change in the environment, species don't have time adapt. That's what creates a crisis.[xxxiii]

Coach Ken: Gotcha! We just think differently, I don't think we have a crisis.

Then someone Alex did not know chimed in:

Mr. IKnowMoreThanYou: Science shouldn't be politicized. Climate change is just a redistribution of wealth scheme by globalists wanting to take over the world. Just this week 30,000 scientists agreed that there was NO CLIMATE CRISIS.

Alex had been here before. So many people repost claims of scientific evidence where there is little to no proof behind their claims. It's this behavior that makes fake news such an effective weapon against the truth. In this case, a simple check on Snopes fact checking website gave her all the information she needed.

Alex: Mr. IKnowMoreThanYou, Check out www.snopes.com/3000-scientists-reject.../ FACT CHECK: Did 30,000 Scientists Declare Climate Change a Hoax?

Neither did this happen last week as you say, nor was it 30,000 scientists. Additionally, it wasn't validated at all. It was a public petition. Please try to understand what science is and what it is not.

Then Coach Ken piled on.

Coach Ken: I didn't say I was right. Nor did I say you were wrong. I just stated what I believe. What's wrong with that?

Alex: Coach Ken, you are just playing semantics and wasting my time. Believe what you want, be an ostrich. Side with people who don't understand the difference between peer-reviewed science vs a petition. I'll stick with science.

Coach Ken: You are trolling me, not the other way around.

Alex: Coach Ken, true it's your wall and your post, but look up the definition of a troll. I wasn't being disrespectful or off topic. I guess your command of English matches your command of science. OK now I am being disrespectful.

Then she posted the definition of an Internet troll as provided by Google:

```
In Internet slang, a troll is a person who
starts quarrels or upsets people on the
Internet to distract and sow discord by posting
inflammatory and digressive, [1] extraneous, or
off-topic messages in an online community (such
```

as a newsgroup, forum, chat room, or blog) with
the intent of provoking readers into displaying
emotional responses[2] and normalizing
tangential discussion,[3] whether for the
troll's amusement or a specific gain.

Alex was wasting too much time. She clicked unfriend on Coach
Ken. Alex understood the power of Facebook and how naïve
computer scientists thought giving everyone a voice is a good
thing, but as Stan Lee said, "With great power comes great
responsibility."

It was clear to Alex like many freedoms that people in the
United States had, that many people couldn't use that liberty
responsibly. People are trusted not to drink and drive, yet thirty
people a day die from drunk drivers. At least with drinking and
driving people have to pass a modicum of tests to prove they
have the basic skills required to drive before getting a license.
What particularly irked Alex was the blatant irresponsibility of
many gun owners and that in many cases they are not required
to complete training or even register their weapons.

Just then she got a hit, Antonio's email came in.

OMG, is this a joke? What do I need to do? Call
me 52-753 533 1212.

Antonio.

Alex had no intension to call. She had baited people with this
trick before. Instead she paused for ten minutes to make him
sweat and then sent the following email.

Antonio,

We've attached a series of photos in a power
point presentation to show you that your
daughter is alive and well. For now.

She left it at that. Alex knew there was no way that he could resist, especially with no further action requested. The PowerPoint had a virus installed within it and when Antonio opened it, it would most likely infect his computer.

CHAPTER TWENTY-SEVEN

Staring up at the bridge was horrifying. Nine victims were hung from their necks for all to see. Some of the bodies were men, others were women. Neither sex was spared the disgrace of being dangled from above with duct tape over their faces, half naked, and with their hands bound. It wasn't enough to kill the enemy; disgrace was part of the treatment.

Cartel violence was no longer an event in the shadows. Now it was glorified and publicized for all to see. A banner was hung to ensure there was no doubt about their menacing message.

As Miguel described the scene to Mark Belcastro he felt like he was back in Mexico, surrounded by the drug wars. "It was horrible," he explained to Mark. "And that wasn't all of it. Later in the day, ten more heads were found in coolers. They just dumped them by city hall with another note."[xxxiv]

"Looking at their hacked-up bodies, I couldn't even imagine what tortures they must have endured before ultimately being put out of their misery with a bullet." Gang and cartel violence was the new norm people attempted to tolerate on a daily basis, but this new violence wasn't something that people could become callused to.

"Were the cartels responsible, the same one's that threatened you to join?" asked Belcastro.

"Well no, but it doesn't matter. They'll make you do unspeakable things. MS-13 wanted me to be with them and their motto is "mata, viola, controla."[xxxv]

Belcastro wasn't fluent in Spanish, "What does that mean?"

"Kill, rape, control. Do you think I can be a part of that? What would my daughter think if she knew I was part of a gang?"

Miguel knew, whoever you join with, eventually someone will come for you. Then he had a horrible thought, *"How does he not know the motto of MS-13?"* and asked Belcastro, "How long have you been an immigration attorney?"

Belcastro paused, a bit surprised that Miguel would question his experience, "Well, I've been a criminal attorney for over 20 years."

Miguel didn't want to cause trouble, but having to retell the horrors of where he was from heightened his paranoia. "That's a lot of criminal experience, but what about representing undocumented immigrants?"

"Well, to be completely honest, you are only my third case, but the other two are coming along nicely. Don't worry, the law is the law and I know the judge from previous cases," explained Belcastro. The truth was his criminal practice was struggling and given the change in political climate, the number of desperate people in need of an immigration lawyer was too inviting to reject the opportunity.

Miguel did not look convinced. There was a very uncomfortable pause before Belcastro broke the silence, "Well, we need to focus on your case at hand Miguel. If you want to hire another attorney, that is your right, but your aunt has already paid me to handle your case and from what I understand you wouldn't have money to hire another. Trust me, we can get this done. What you describe is horrible. No one should have to live through what you did and certainly your daughter doesn't deserve to be separated from her only parent."

Belcastro knew how to manipulate and push his clients' buttons. By bringing Miguel's daughter up, Miguel would cave.

Miguel wished his aunt could have attended the meeting, but with money so tight, there was no way she could take another day off from work. She had already lost a day due to the bond hearing. With no viable alternative, Miguel had to move forward with Belcastro. "What else do you need to know?" asked Miguel.

"We need to create a list of atrocities that will paint a picture that it is unsafe for you to return home and build your case from there."

Miguel didn't want to think about it, but he had to "When I was younger, my friend Jefe's mom was literally scalped with a machete. They cut her down while we were in just across the street. I still have nightmares about it."

"My god, that's horrible," Belcastro was genuinely disturbed. "Did you witness it firsthand?"

"Thankfully, not. But we walked into the house right after and found her body in a puddle of blood. Her body was still twitching, and my friend collapsed screaming and sobbing over her body." Miguel made a cross over his heart, looked up to the ceiling and gave a silent prayer for his friend.

"It was then that the threats came. The next day I was told if I didn't join the gang, they would do the same to my mother. I had no choice. But my mother made plans to get me out of the country right after that. She sold everything she could to get the money for the coyotes."

Belcastro was almost afraid to ask, "And your mother? How is she now?"

"She's fine. Once I was gone, there was very little reason other than revenge to bother her."

"Well when Judge Gaudet hears all of this, I am confident you will not be going anywhere. We'll be meeting up with him in your master hearing in a week." Belcastro finished gathering the rest of the data he needed to file the paperwork and then sent Miguel on his way.

CHAPTER TWENTY-EIGHT

Alex was far more apt to call in with good news. Given that all three new attempts hit pay dirt, she figured it was a reasonable time to check in.

Alex dialed Vinny's administrative assistant, "Hey it's Agent Pinto, is Vincente there?"

"Yes, hold please." Cathy was always so professional, never one to make small talk.

"Hey Alex, I assume you have good news if you are calling this early in the week," Vincente said cheerfully.

"You know it. In addition to all the other hacks, I've just speared three more. Batting 1000 today," Alex said with pride.

"Well that's great, but how are we doing with cracking the real target's accounts?" asked Vincente.

"I'm still working on that. I was hoping to get to his administrative assistant's account, but she hasn't bitten on anything yet." Alex said with little enthusiasm.

"Do you have her personal cell number yet?"

"Actually, yes I was able to pull that the other day." Alex said with a little more pride.

"Did you check for any known vulnerabilities with her phone?" Vinnie knew the single easiest way into a phone was exploiting a known security flaw in the phone. Unfortunately for users, when either hackers or cyber security experts discovered a flaw in a phone's security there was a delay before the manufacturer could push out a patch. During that sweet spot time in between leaves phones open for attack. While Apple users like to think they are always secure, they are just as vulnerable to these types of breeches as anyone else.

"Is the Pope catholic? Of course, I did," replied Alex.

"Don't keep me in suspense, is she vulnerable?"

"Unfortunately, not at all. Her phone is completely up to date."

"Let's go nuclear."

"I was going to give it a little more time, but you've got it. That's why you are the Grand Poobah, I'll get right on it."

Alex hung up and pulled up Belinda Gómez's cell phone number from her database. If she wanted generically hacked accounts, she wouldn't even have to go deep into the dark web, she could go to any number of websites like OGUsers.com where they sold hacked account information from social media accounts with strong followings.

However, for a case like this she needed the help of someone with access to cellular providers' internal tools. Hackers that have gained access to them weren't about to make that sort of access public, but every good white hat had their share of resources and Alex was no different.

Alex contacted Groys Banister via Signal App. In addition to encrypting messages back and forth, messages weren't stored on a central server where they could be subpoenaed later. Signal wasn't the only secure app, other apps like WhatsApp claim to be as secure. In many cases they may use the same secure protocols, but very few techies trust what a closed-sourced application like WhatsApp may do with information behind the scenes. In contrast, Signal was an open source project, so paranoid minds could check for themselves that nothing inappropriate was being done with the data beyond the public's watchful eye.

Signal also had the benefit of not tying a phone number to the account. While you needed a number to set the account up, it was only used once upon registration and could be discarded afterwards. Alex had plenty of burner phones / SIMs for just that purpose.

Alex used her pseudonym, NightWidow, when interacting with Groys. She always had fun making up aliases as well as guessing the meaning of others. Groys' handle was actually Yiddish for Great User.

Alex had a standing agreement. She wired him $200 in the most prolific virtual currency, Bitcoin, and texted him a phone number and a new sim card number which she wanted the phone number transferred to. In exchange, he would provide the information to redirect Belinda's phone number to Alex's new sim.

NightWidow: You online?

GroysBanister: Always.

NightWidow: Phone #: 52-753 533 7742

NightWidow: Sim: 89 334 88 0417 00 012345 1

After a few minutes pause, back came the information.

Home Address: Av. Paseo de la Reforma 439, Cuauhtémoc, 06500 Ciudad de México, CDMX, Mexico

IMSI number: 990000862471854

Special Instructions: My favorite teacher is Señora Garcia.

That was all she needed to call the wireless provider and switch control of her phone to her burner phone. However, if she simjacked the phone in the middle of the day, it was likely Belinda would notice and there would be little time to work with the hacked accounts. Instead, she waited until Belinda was likely to be asleep.

Alex settled in to catch up on some Netflix, but set her phone alarm for 1:00 AM just in case she passed out mid-show.

CHAPTER TWENTY-NINE

Miguel made sure he wasn't just on time, but an hour early arriving to the courthouse. There was no way he wanted to add any additional negative connotation to his case, nor did he want to risk his aunt not receiving a refund for the bond.

The wait for his case to be called was as interminable as the first time around. While he waited, Miguel went over the notes he took from his conversations with Belcastro.

Once it was his turn and once all the formalities were through, Judge Gaudet turned to Belcastro and asked the question that he already knew the answer to, "What form of relief will Mr. Lopez be applying for?"

Belcastro simply replied, "Asylum, Your Honor."

Then Judge Gaudet asked, "Is Mr. Lopez concerned with the clock?"

"Indeed, he is Your Honor. He is looking to apply for an employment authorization so he can continue to support his lovely daughter as well as help with his aunt's expenses," Belcastro stated.

Miguel heard his lawyer parrot the words they discussed when preparing for the trial, but he really didn't understand the ramifications of their answers to the judge's questions. "You have to trust Mr. Belcastro," Aunt Rosa kept telling him.

Miguel was literally putting his life in Belcastro's hands. Most seasoned lawyers would declare they were not concerned with the clock. This would slow the court proceedings down by considerable time, often extending it by years. The downside of stating you weren't concerned with the clock was that you couldn't get work authorization papers. Most clients didn't care, they would just work under the table.

As uncomfortable as it was when his lawyer was responding, when the DHS lawyer Ms. Burnett addressed him it was far worse. "Mr. Lopez, as I am sure you are aware, you were supposed to apply for asylum when you first entered the United States, but you didn't do that. Why are you applying now?" she asked.

Miguel thought to himself, *"Well because I got caught, cabrón."*

Miguel took a deep breath and remembered his coaching from Belcastro, "Your honor, conditions were terrible when I left Mexico as a young boy. My mother rushed me out of the country when I was threatened to join a gang. I didn't know what the ramifications were to these actions. I didn't have any council at the time and didn't know I had to apply."

"However, it's much worse now. I've talked with my mother and the violence by gangs and cartels near my home is horrible. They have no shame or humility in what they do. It's all out in the open. Your Honor, I don't want to be forced into a life of violence and crime. I'm a good man. I'm a good father," Miguel continued.

Judge Gaudet pondered the evidence in front of him for what felt like hours to Miguel. In reality, it was just a few minutes. "OK, given that you are concerned with the clock, we will get you scheduled for an individual merits hearing next month."

"Geez, that's fast," thought Miguel. Belcastro told him it can take up to 180 days for the courts to schedule the hearing.

Belcastro could see the fear in Miguel's eyes, "Don't worry, we got this."

The judge dismissed them. As they walked out, Miguel asked, "Mr. Belcastro, do you still think I'll be able to stay in the United States?"

"Absolutely. Judge Gaudet has always been very lenient in his sentencing. I think when he weighs all that you have said he'll grant you asylum. That's why I think he rushed to schedule your merit hearing. We were lucky to get him," reassured Belcastro.

CHAPTER THIRTY

Alex awoke to the not so melodical alarm of her phone. While she could set it to something less abrasive, like the *Imperial March* from *Star Wars*, she preferred an old fashioned buzz to jolt her out of a deep sleep.

Alex had her routine. Unlike many hackers that lived on 5-hour ENERGY or high sugar / caffeine drinks, she preferred a more scientific and long term approach. She didn't drink calories. Instead, she drank high end teas, like DAVIDsTEA coffee pu'erh or their hot chocolate tea. They had about half the caffeine of coffee, but when consumed over a longer period of time and with unprocessed foods like nuts, provided a sustained energy boost to work through the night.

It didn't take her long to rouse and get down to work. "OK, let's have at it," thought Alex.

She called T-Mobile and navigated the incessant menus to get to a live person. Until, finally, success.

"Hello, welcome to T-Mobile. Let's Talk! How can I help you?" said a woman with an Indian accent.

Alex pondered that even in Mexico, cheaper labor was sought, but she focused on the task at hand. Alex played the Master Thespian stating in a semi hysterical voice, "I can't believe how careless I was, I dropped my phone in the toilet. I have an old phone here that I need to connect to my phone number. Can you help me?"

"Of course, that's why we are here. Can you please supply me with your full name as it appears on the account?" asked the representative.

"Oh yes, it's Belinda Gómez," Alex quickly replied.

"And the address on the account?"

Alex recited the address provided by GroysBanister.

The agent continued to check off her list of questions, "And can you provide your password, it's a favorite teacher."

Alex always pondered why they give out hints to passwords, if it's supposed to be a secure password wouldn't it make sense not to? "That would be my third grade teacher, Señora Garcia. She was the best!"

The operator stuck to her script. "Perfect, all I need now is your IMSI number."

Alex wondered if people in India had grade school as she did, but focused on her goal, "990000862471854."

"Let me put you on a brief hold while I provision your new, well, old phone."

After about a one minute pause, she came back. "You are all done. Is there anything else I can help you with?"

Alex was beaming, "Nope, appreciate all the help. She now had control of Belinda's phone number.

She started with resetting her email account passwords, including Belinda's work email. Once in, it was a cakewalk. One by one she went through her various accounts and requested password resets. Many accounts had two-factor authentication, requiring that she verify her identity by replying to a text message.

While messages were being sent from various accounts, they were now all going to Alex instead of Belinda. Even if Belinda was awake, it would be unlikely she would notice anything was wrong until she tried to make a call or access data. Still, Alex needed to work quickly and get what she needed before getting caught. Opportunities like this wouldn't happen twice for the same person.

Targets like a CEO's administrative assistant were often back doors into a corporation's network. While the CEO of a tech company wasn't as likely to fall for social engineering tactics, a relatively uneducated and maybe technologically-challenged assistant was much easier prey.

The first and most important step was to download all of Belinda's corporate email. If Belinda discovered the ruse, Alex could be cut off quickly. Once the data was stored locally, Alex knew she could mine it for pertinent information at her leisure later.

She opened a Microsoft Outlook client, logged in like anyone else would, but then drilled into the `Account Settings` and then deeper into `Offline Settings`. She switched the amount of time to `All` and smiled as the inbox started filling up.

Just then there was a knock on the door. "Did I hear you say you dropped your phone in the toilet?" ask her mom. Her mom was a notoriously light sleeper. Alex was never able to sneak back into the house past curfew without getting caught. Things never changed.

"Um, sorry I woke you," Alex paused. "Well, you did hear me say that, but no I was joking with my friend. Can we talk later, I'm in the middle of a game."

Alex's mom bought it and left her alone. Alex wondered if she would ever come clean with her parents about her job. They probably thought she was a disappointment, but that was all part of the deal she made when signing up.

CHAPTER THIRTY-ONE

Mark Belcastro fired up his Keurig, for what wouldn't be the last time that night. The ability to brew one cup at a time, especially now that they had coffee that was double dosed with caffeine, got him through many a long night of trial preparations. As his cup filled with steamy goodness he could hear his secretary screeching at him, "Mark, you know those containers are horrible for the environment!" She even went as far as buying him reusable K-cups for Christmas, but he couldn't let the environment get in the way of productivity.

If he had years of experience with immigration law, he'd already have canned reports for each country a client came from and could just pull out all sorts of horrific statistics and stories relating to the atrocities from their country of origin. However, his previous two cases were from El Salvador and Guatemala, the source of many of the caravans highlighted in the news. He needed fresh facts for Mexico.

Belcastro started with a report from Amnesty International. He knew the rough outline of what he would find before he ever started to read the summary of the reports. The news was filled with mass killings, beheadings and once safe tourist locations were plagued with crime. When he dove into the report he was appalled at the statistics that backed the headlines.

The reports started with a few quotes that only reinforced the feelings of every migrant,

"Every person has the right to seek safety: this is a moment that will prove itself infamous, when the country turned its back on those it used to welcome and chose to ignore people's humanity."[xxxvi]

Even though Belcastro was mainly in it for the money, he did have a heart. It always amazed him how the country once welcomed the tired masses, but once those masses rested up and got situated in the United States they forgot their previous plight and cast dispersions on the next generation of immigrants. This was true back to the 1850's when ill feelings were felt toward those that looked different like Chinese people. This eventually led to an outright ban of Chinese immigrants. It was even true for people that looked similar, but practiced a different form of Christianity. The Irish Catholics weren't particularly welcome in the east coast cities where they settled.

"What happened to our country?" thought Belcastro. He remembered as a child when boats entering from Cuba would enter our waters and be welcomed with open arms. *"When did we become so heartless?"*

The complete Amnesty International report for 2017/2018 was more than 400 pages. *"Thank God there's an index."* Belcastro clicked down to Mexico with the first stat jumping off the page being the new annual record for homicides that were registered: 42,583. Belcastro knew from previous research that the US' homicide total was over 15,000. "Geez, that makes Mexico have almost three times as many homicides, with only about a third of the population."

Belcastro decided to dig deeper. Given Mexico City's reputation for violence, he figured it would be easy to find stats that were even worse than the country in general. A quick Google turned up a Wikipedia page highlighting the fifty worst cities in the world. Unfortunately, for Miguel's case, Mexico City wasn't in the top 50. Mexico had plenty of representation though with five of the worst six cities in the world flying a Mexican flag.[xxxvii]

Belcastro dug deeper finding an article in the *Mexico News Daily* showing the recent surge in homicides. It was dated 2018. *"Good enough."*xxxviii

Back to the Amnesty report, Belcastro read about the continual problem of arbitrary arrests and detentions. While he had issues with isolated law enforcement over his criminal career, he generally respected the people serving to protect his community. Mexico was a different story. According to the report, young men living in poverty were a target. *"Excellent. Something else I can use,"* thought Belcastro.

If all of that wasn't enough, the next section of the report focused on "Torture and other ill-treatment." It was concluded that regardless of the new laws passed, problems were still pervasive.

Missing people, check. There were almost 35,000 people known to be missing with the actual number suspected to be much higher. Cases were just one offs. In one incident 43 students went forcibly missing. *"Geez, this wasn't some far off place like the girls in Nigeria that were kidnapped by Boko Haram, this was our neighbor,"* thought Belcastro. The official Mexican government story was that the missing students were all dead and burned in a trash heap. This theory was dismissed scientifically by an Interdisciplinary Group of Independent Experts, so the case remains unsolved.

Belcastro skipped past the brutalities against women and girls, migrants, and the LGBTQ community. Facing the horrific reality Miguel would face was more than enough to stomach for one evening. He didn't want to look any further.

The last section of the report gave him some good information to highlight the economic hardships caused by the earthquakes.

With that, Belcastro called it a night, content that he had the ammunition needed to prove that Miguel couldn't safely return to Mexico City.

CHAPTER THIRTY-TWO

While the email account was downloading, Alex scraped as much data as she could from the social media accounts. That information might be useful for other spearfishing attacks as well as drawing the full picture of all the players. However, it was the work email account that was the coveted trophy.

To not raise suspicion, she next went about making the hack look less targeted and diabolical. She wanted to make the attack appear like it was just another social media hack.

She scheduled a story for an hour later on Facebook:

```
Trump Won the both the Electoral Vote and the
POPULAR vote. Voter fraud is rampant. Don't
trust…
```

On Instagram she scheduled:

```
Latest Flu vaccine leads to orange skin and
small hands.
```

Then she scheduled three tweets:

```
FDA no longer effective at preventing
salmonella.
```

```
Reagan family sues President Trump for stealing
slogan Make America Great Again.
```

```
Clinton behind latest mass shooting. Lock her
up!
```

By creating posts through the target's social media accounts, the target would think they were hacked like countless others to be hijacked for social media warfare and there would be little reason to suspect that the real target of the hack was the corporate email account. As she finished setting up the posts the download completed. For good measure Alex flooded Belinda's messenger list with an annoying text stating to click on the video, a video that had the photo of the recipient, and asked, is this you? The video actually advertised herbal Viagra.

It didn't really matter what the fake news stories were. She had to admit, it did give her pleasure to flood fake news on the accounts of the very people propagating it across the Internet.

Alex now focused on the download. She already had a program written to check for certain buzzwords, because manually checking every email would have taken too long. She also uploaded the data to Homeland Security's network where a more powerful array of computers could apply machine learning techniques where it performed a more sophisticated natural language match based on previously flagged emails and a control group of innocuous emails like ones about buying a daughter a present.

It wasn't long before her program struck gold. It highlighted an email with the subject p*ssw*rd. Attached was a file containing account numbers and a few passwords for her boss, Jeremiah Lechtenberg. It even contained his house's alarm code.

Alex wasted no time. She immediately logged into Lectenberg's account and started a similar download process as she had with Belinda's. She was too anxious to wait for it to complete and started manually sifting through his emails.

Starting from the top she saw he was having a fight with his wife. A few emails down she also saw he was having a fight with his girlfriend. *"Should I be cruel and forward an email from his girlfriend to his wife,"* she thought.

"Generous!" as she saw gift receipts for both his wife and girlfriend.

There were plenty of iniquitous emails related to bug reports, project plans and employee hires.

She then found links to their cloud-based accounting system. She tried the same email address and password, but to not avail.

"Hopefully, he's not up," she thought as she requested a password reset. When the email came in, she quickly clicked on the link, reset his password and then removed the reset password email as well as the confirmation of it from his email account. He would probably still get a notification on his phone, but the less evidence the better.

Alex logged into the accounting system and found references to invoices totaling hundreds of millions of dollars. She downloaded all of them and uploaded them to Homeland Security servers so they could work their magic. Even if Lechtenberg discovered the breach, she had the data she was after.

Alex looked over at the clock, 3:00 AM. She had better get some sleep, she had to travel back home to Virginia and check in at the home office later in the day.

CHAPTER THIRTY-THREE

Alex's parents drove her to the local train station in Woodcrest, NJ. From there she commuted to 30th Street Station where she picked up an Amtrak train to DC. It was a commute she made many times. She tucked herself into a cozy seat hoping no one would sit next to her. She turned on her hot spot, which worked more reliably and with better performance than the free Amtrak Wi-Fi. As tired as she was she wasn't really planning on getting "work" done, but had lots of emails and social media to catch up on.

Just as she settled in, an overweight businessman wearing a loud 80s style red, power tie. "Hi there young lady," he said.

Alex politely, returned the hello as she hit the privacy button on her laptop.

"I'm Lawrence. Are you headed all the way to D.C.?" he inquired.

Alex was not in the mood for a Chatty Cathy, "Yes, I assume you are as well?"

"Yes, I have a meeting with some representatives."

"Sure you do. Probably a lobbyist," thought Alex.

He fired up his computer and Alex couldn't help the curiosity to see what he was logging into.

The rotund man's pudgy fingers navigated to the National Review website, a conservative magazine/website with about 100,000 subscribers. *"Ugh, just as I suspected."*

Alex decided to have some fun. "Um sir, I wouldn't do that!" she warned before he actually clicked login.

"What do you mean? I can read whatever I want."

"Well of course, I'm a member of the National Review as well," replied Alex. Of course, she was lying, but he would have no way to know.

"Well then what's the problem?" he asked.

"I'm a comp sci professional, and if you worked with me, I'd tell you to never store passwords like that." Alex pointed to the stored password on the computer screen that was obfuscated.

"Why is that an issue, I made sure it was a complex password before I saved it." Sensing Alex was a friend and conservative, he extended his hand, "Nice to meet you."

She shook his hand and replied, "Alex. It's not an issue of what the password is, it's that it's easy to have it stolen. Want me to show you?"

Lawrence didn't know what to think, but an attractive, fit young woman showing him attention was hard to turn down. "Sure."

She didn't wait for him to have second thoughts and rotating his laptop in her direction. "Watch this!"

She went into Chromes developer tools, right clicked to inspect the password field, drilled down through a bunch of HTML/CSS code, and then changed the text where it described the field as a password to `TEXT`.

Instantly, Lawrence's password showed on the screen. `TrumpIs*urS@vi*r`. *"Got ya,"* she thought committing it to memory.

"See, if you walk away for your computer for a second, anyone can hack into it," she explained.

"Well, um thanks!" Robert responded not knowing what to say.

"You're welcome, always happy to help. I guess with a password like that you weren't a big Obama fan." Alex really had a good percentage of devil inside her. She couldn't help but bait Lawrence.

"Don't get me started on that N..," Lawrence caught himself just in time and finished his thought, "ninnyhammer."

"Who uses words like that? He must have thought of it before to cover his racist beliefs," thought Alex. She was ready for some fun indeed. "Well under Obama we certainly had great economic prosperity, you can't really argue with the growth in the stock market and jobs creation to this day."

Lawrence took the bait, "I don't know about that, but what I do know is he wants to take credit for everyone's business success."

"What?" was all Alex could respond with. She's heard a lot of criticisms of Obama, but this was a new one.

"Oh, I am sure you conveniently missed when Barack Hussein Obama said 'If you've got a business, you didn't build that. Somebody else made that happen,'" Lawrence said with a beaming smile like he snared Alex in a trap.

Alex hated how conservatives always seemed to call President Obama, by his full name, emphasizing the Hussein, and skipping the title of President. Given that a poll showed two-thirds of voters that approved of Trump still believed President Obama was Muslim.

"Oh yeah, I remember that. Funny, I didn't take it the way you do. See I went to school for computer science. In order to be an effective programmer we have to use the Internet every day.

The Internet was started by a government program. It led to a single standard that everyone communicates on. Without the government, we would have had a hundred companies peddling their own communication system like AOL online or CompuServe. None of the systems would talk to each other and we'd be light years behind where we are today. So, what Obama meant was the government helps to provide an infrastructure far beyond our system of roads to help businesses flourish. Does your business use roads and the Internet?" Alex asked and then realized she missed the best opportunity; they were riding on a federally subsidized Amtrak train.

"Well yeah, of course we use those things."

Alex pressed further, "So what's the nature of your business?"

Lawrence was always one willing to boast about his family's educational empire. "My brothers and I started a series of Montessori schools and now we have ten of them."

"Wow, that's impressive. Was your family born with a silver spoon? That had to be expensive to start," Alex replied trying to keep a straight face.

"We started with one and it was expensive. My brothers and I had saved about $150 grand, borrowed another hundred from our parents and the SBA matched it with a loan. We took that one school and grew it to where we are today."

"So, the government provided the infrastructure for your business." Alex turned out to be the one closing the trap.

Lawrence genuinely thought about what Alex said. She watched as he momentarily debated with himself. Then Lawrence concluded, "No, I totally disagree. My brothers and I are solely responsible for building our business."

Alex knew she was just wasting time and politely dismissed the conversation. "I've actually got to do some work, but it was nice chatting."

Alex went back to what she was doing before, but planned to keep an eye on his computer to grab his Facebook ID. Odds were that he used the same password for all his accounts and wasn't likely to have changed it by then. She planned to leave him a little surprise on his wall later after she was off the train. Perhaps a meme about Sarah Palin, *Miss Family Values*, divorce. "*Family values* candidate Sarah Palin is getting a divorce, and I can see irony from my house."

CHAPTER THIRTY-FOUR

Today was the day. Miguel awoke, but was still in a trancelike state. Not just his life, but his daughter and aunt's would all be inexplicitly altered by the outcome of the trial. Belcastro had reassured him he had this, but Miguel knew too many people that entered court confident only to have any hubris melted away by a strict judge.

When the time came for Miguel to step before the judge with his lawyer he was still in a funk he couldn't shake. Fortunately, he didn't have to say much as the judge directed most questions to Belcastro directly.

His lawyer recounted the detailed statistics he gathered as well as horrific stories of gun violence. Miguel tuned them out and just iterated on what life would be like if he had to return to Mexico. He couldn't touch his Julia again, no scent of her baby shampoo, and her smile would be limited to a video chat. *"Would Julia ever forgive me?"* thought Miguel.

Then he was brought back to reality, "Mr. Lopez, will you please answer the question?"

"I am sorry sir, I mean Your Honor. What was the question again?" Miguel asked.

The lawyer for DHS repeated her statement, "Mr. Lopez, it's a simple question. Have you ever been arrested, anywhere in the world?"

"Well yes, of course. I was arrested by ICE," Miguel said as innocently as possible. *"Was this a trick question? Of course, they know I was arrested why else would I be here?"*

"Let me be more explicit. Were you arrested anytime, anywhere other than when ICE picked you up for being in the country illegally?"

Miquel paused. Then responded, "No, I am a good man."

Ms. Burnett figured Miguel would deny it. In fact, she was counting on it, "Mr. Lopez, your record is not as clean as you implied. Before you left Mexico, we have evidence that you were involved in a grocery store robbery in which the shop owner was injured."

Miguel went ghost white, *"How do they know about that?"*

Belcastro jumped to his feet, "Your honor, I object. Why wasn't I informed of this evidence?"

The judge turned his attention to Ms. Burnett, but he had seen this scenario play out many times before. "We just retrieved this information from INTERPOL yesterday Your Honor. We only found this information based on a search when we retook Mr. Lopez's fingerprints."

Unfortunately for Miguel, blindsides like this were common and while Belcastro was used to the rules of traditional criminal court, this was not criminal court. Here they were not required to present evidence in advance as in a customary reciprocal arrangement.

We would like to hand this in as evidence," the Ms. Burnett replied with a sense of smugness as she knew Miguel lost all credibility by lying in court.

"I will permit it," Judge Gaudet ruled as the documents were passed to Belcastro and then an additional copy to the judge.

Belcastro was flabbergasted, "As I am just seeing this for the first time. I'd like continuance. I need to review it with my client."

The judge was tired of hearing sob cases only to find out there was a criminal background. When defendants were dishonest in his courtroom it changed his demeanor dramatically. Gaudet lost his sympathetic edge, "Over your objection I am going to admit it into evidence."

Ms. Burnett continued, "Do you deny that you participated in the crime?"

Miguel looked to Belcastro in fear. Belcastro looked back in frustration. "Do not look to your lawyer to answer the question Mr. Lopez. Look at me!" Judge Gaudet demanded.

"Um, Your Honor. It wasn't my fault. I was forced to do that just before I left Mexico. They said they would shoot my mother if I didn't comply. That's why my mother got me out. I didn't want to be part of a gang like that," Miguel pleaded.

"And what was your excuse for not telling the court about this earlier? Did someone else have a gun to your head?" Judge Gaudet replied with a tone of sarcasm.

"No, Your Honor."

Miguel knew he had messed up. If he had told Belcastro in advance maybe he could have framed the incident better. His thoughts drifted to what his knew life was likely to be like.

Belcastro kicked him under the table to get his attention back as the judge was wrapping up, "Mr. Lopez, while your pleas are credible, I am afraid they do not rise to the level that would grant you asylum. The case made before me is applicable to most of the population of most countries. However, the law is the law and you clearly violated it. You entered the country without presenting yourself for asylum. Your lawyer did not make a compelling case why you are personally in such danger that you could not return to Mexico."

Gaudet continued, in a robotic voice that has said these words over and over again, "I've heard all your testimony and evidence; I am denying your application for withholding and removal and convention against torture. I am now moving to the decision phase of your case and you are not eligible for applying for asylum. I am entering an order for your removal to Mexico."

Miguel knew that this could be the outcome and deep down knew it was the likely outcome.

The reality sunk in for Miguel as the judge stated, "As such, you have 30 days to file an appeal. If you do not file, you must leave the United States and return to Mexico. When you arrive, you must document your arrival with the US consulates in Mexico City. When the documentation of your arrival reaches us, your aunt can eventually receive a refund of the bond. If you fail to do so, not only will she forfeit her money, but you will also be ineligible to reapply for asylum for ten years regardless of changes in your situation or the political climate."

The judge now directed his attention away from Miguel, "Mr. Belcastro, this is not criminal court. I suggest you study the case history of immigration law in more detail before I see you again in my courtroom."

Miguel and Belcastro walked out of the courtroom together. Before Miguel could say a word, Belcastro dug into him, "How could you let that 'little' detail slip and forget to mention it to me?"

Miguel had enough of being polite, "Are you kidding me? The judge just berated you and you're coming at me?"

Belcastro had no patience for Miguel, "I told you at the start you had to be completely honest and forthright with me. Were you?" He didn't give Miguel time to answer, "No!"

Miguel was crushed. He didn't know what to think or do, but then his Aunt Rosa approached and gave him a much needed hug. "I guess we could hire another lawyer for an appeal," Miguel offered.

Aunt Rosa froze, her warm touch no longer felt as comforting.

"What is it Auntie?" asked Miguel.

"It's not that simple. I don't know how to tell you this easily, but I have to return your bond money within two months or they are going to take the house."

"What?" Previously, every time Miguel had brought up the topic of where the money for his bond came from Aunt Rosa changed the topic.

"I didn't want to worry you. You had enough to be concerned with," pleaded Aunt Rosa.

Miguel asked, "Where did it come from?"

"It's enough to say that it came from people you don't want to not return it to. I have two months to make good."

The last thing Miguel wanted was allow his family to be harmed further by his actions. "Well that pretty much settles it. We have to make sure you get your money back and the only way to do that is for me to go back to Mexico. There's no time to request an appeal and get you your money back," reasoned Miguel.

Aunt Rosa didn't want to admit the truth "There has to be another way!"

"I wish there were. Let's head home. It's been a very hard day." Miguel thought, *"Well at least it is home for now,"* but the clock was ticking.

CHAPTER THIRTY-FIVE

By the time Alex returned to Virginia, a significant amount of her data was analyzed. As was standard practice, the various dimensions of information found in one investigation were cross referenced with information from other active, and sometimes non-active, investigations.

As Alex was driving into the office, Alex received a text, which her car read to her.

```
"Incoming Message from Vinnie. Interesting
correlations found. Gathering the team to meet
you upon your arrival. Great work."
```

Memex and other automated tools Homeland Security used could correlate data and highlight areas of interest but ultimately it took human eyes to draw the conclusions.

Alex arrived and went directly to her desk for the first time in weeks. As she approached, there was a gift waiting for her. It was a piece of asphalt with the top of a running trophy laying horizontal on it. Head down on the *road*. *"Very funny guys,"* thought Alex.

Alex was a good sport, but turnabout was fair play. Alex knew it was either Tano or Traya who pulled off the shenanigans. Harmless practical jokes were their calling card. It required immediate retribution.

After fiddling with her computer for a few minutes, Alex walked up to Traya and Tano. "Good one guys. Want to see a video of the actual event?" She pulled out a USB key and popped it into Traya's computer.

"It's the video entitled *TheGreatFall.mpg*," volunteered Alex.

They all had a good laugh as Alex relived her faceplanting, but Alex would have the last laugh. With the hubris from their stunt, they didn't expect Alex would move so quickly. She placed a small program she wrote that randomly repositions the mouse's position on the screen at unspecified time intervals. It was a program Alex wrote in college to punk on her friends. Every now and then she was more than happy to bring it back to life.

Alex set the initial delay to take a week. *"I'll be out of the office when that one triggers. It will drive him crazy!"* Alex thought to herself.

With the *important* work for national security completed, they headed to the conference room to meet up with Vinnie and a few junior analysts.

"Welcome back Alex," greeted Vinny.

"Good to be back. Let's see what we got!" Alex was curious to see what they turned up.

Vinny popped on one of the large monitors in the room and pulled up a graph showing typical Memex output. At the top was a node labeled DataRex. It branched out to numerous nodes labeled for companies with whom they had contracts. Those companies in turn branched to other companies, but the splintering then primarily stopped. Instead, the next level of lines all aggregated into three entities. DataRex didn't have as many clients as they appeared to have.

The three entities were all super PACs. Since Citizens for Truth, Americans For Truth, and Truth for All were created as Super PACs they weren't limited by how they could receive funds. Thanks to the Citizens United ruling from the Supreme Court which equated donations to PAC an extension of the right to freedom of speech, PACs didn't have individual limits on donations. Superficially this sounds like a reasonable extension of the Constitution. However, like many actions there were unforeseen, or maybe intentional, consequences. By equating corporations as people, dark money could now be donated in unlimited quantities and easily from foreign sources.[xxxix]

"I think we all know what this means," Vinny declared. DataRex was a pawn in the giant political game. It wasn't just the Russians that had a hand in manipulating public opinion. DataRex was a giant Fake News producing machine.

Vinny flipped up various heat maps, showing a distribution of fake news stories. While in general they covered the United States, there were many red hot zones indicating greater intensity. Next, Vinny placed an overlay of battleground states on top of them. The pattern was clear. DataRex was targeting battleground states with propaganda.

"The problem is that it's difficult to prosecute someone for fake news," Vinny explained. Given the strength of the first amendment, there's a lot of latitude given to an individual's or company's right to free speech. Some fake news is prosecutable. When the far, far right blogger Alex Jones exaggerated an assault on a 5-year-old child to refugees, stating that pro-refugee yogurt maker Chobani was "caught importing migrant rapists," and that they were responsible for a "500% increase in tuberculosis in Twin Falls" they were sued. They had to print a retraction, but cases like this were the exception not the rule.[xl]

Vinny then flipped on a second monitor. It displayed the work of Traya and Tano. "Now let's look at The Collective's activities," said Vinny. The screen showed an equally complex entanglement of relationships.

"Now here's what's really interesting." Vinny clicked on a `Merge` button. The spider webs combined into a giant entanglement with multiple, overlapping nodes that pulsed to grab the attention of the room.

"So, it would seem that our friends at The Collective are busy with our friends at DataRex," concluded Vinny. "Now, we just need to find out why."

"Guessing you already have a lead on that," Alex prodded Vinny.

Vinny replied, "Well indeed we have. The data from the stingrays are still coming in. We should be ready to report on it shortly."

CHAPTER THIRTY-SIX

Miguel languidly stirred his coffee as his aunt looked on with a worried frown.

She cleared her throat, "You know you have to have 'the' conversation Miguel, you can't keep putting it off."

Miguel stared past his aunt to a family photo on the counter, "There hasn't been time, or the right time. I don't know, lo ciento."

Miguel was close to tears as his aunt approached and put a hand on his shoulder, "Today is your last day," she whispered, "You must talk about it."

Miguel nodded in agreement and continued to endlessly stir his coffee. As he was about to take a sip, he heard the pitter patter of little feet coming down the stairs. "Papa, Buenos Dias!" Julia ran to the kitchen table and jumped into a chair as she enthusiastically did every day before school, "I am ready for breakfast."

Miguel smiled, "Well mi conejita, there is a little change of plans today." Julia looked puzzled but interested. He continued, "I am excusing you from school today because we are going out for a special breakfast and then finally going to the Philadelphia Zoo," he tried to keep his voice from faltering.

Julia squealed with delight, "Papa! Dios Mio! Really?" Her eyes were dancing with joy and she was squirming in her seat.

Miguel smiled, "Yes, so go pack a backpack with some water and snacks and we will go." Julia bounced out of the kitchen with excitement.

Miguel's aunt patted his hand, "You can do this."

He wondered if that was true, "I will, but after the zoo. I want her to have the memory of the day without knowing it might be our last."

Miguel put on Julia's favorite Taylor Swift play list in the car. It didn't appeal to him, but he knew this was all about giving his baby girl everything he could, while he still could.

"Papa, where are we going for desayuno?"

Miguel knew this would be exciting for Julia so he decided not to tell her, "You'll just have to see!"

Julia crossed her arms with a fake pout, she hoped it would be the breakfast spot in Philadelphia that she and her papa always spoke of going to. They were known for their huevos rancheros, a dish with blue corn tortillas topped with a smoky chorizo, lime sour cream, two eggs, spicy guacamole, pepper jack and fried jalapeno pepper. She and her papa joked about who would be able to handle the fried jalapeno. Julia was starting to like spicy food but had never eaten a spicy pepper whole.

As they pulled in Julia broke into a gigantic smile and drew in a breath of air almost in disbelief. "Papa, really, yes?"

It was ironic that a classic American bistro would be famous for a traditional Mexican dish. Many local famous politicians dined here regularly. Miguel wondered if they ever tried it or if they stuck to their boring pancakes, eggs and bacon.

He squeezed her hand, "Let's go have some really great huevos and that fried jalapeno!"

Julia was honestly a little nervous about the pepper, but put a on a brave front, "It's okay if you can't do it, I will eat both of them."

As they approached the door Miguel winced and hoped Julia didn't see the sign. It read, "English only."

As they opened the door they were greeted by the host, a young girl with her straight blond hair pulled back in a long ponytail. She had pearl earrings and a pearl necklace draped around her neck. She instinctively put a hand over her necklace and gave them a lukewarm smile, "May I help you?"

Miguel spoke with authority that he did not feel, "Yes, two for breakfast please."

She gave a curt nod and pulled two menus, "Okay, but I have to tell you that we don't have picture menus here."

Miguel ignored the rub and watched Julia's reaction; he could see the hurt in her eyes.

As they sat down she took her dad's hand, "Papa we can go somewhere else, we don't have to eat here. It's not worth the meanness."

Miguel struggled to find words but was saved by the server who approached quickly. She had some tattoos on her arm and a nose ring, "Welcome, my name is Gina and I will be taking care of you today. Here is some banana bread with maple butter on the house. I hope you will stay and enjoy a nice breakfast with us." Then she whispered with a wink, "I promise we're not all like her here."

Julia smiled and relaxed. Miguel looked at Gina with deep gratitude for the kindness.

They ate without speaking as they excitedly shoveled their upscale meal and slurped their drinks. As they were getting close to finishing their plates Julia piped up, "Well?"

"Well what," Miguel taunted.

Julia giggled, "You know," she pointed to the fried jalapeno still lurking on their plates, mocking them.

Miguel spoke with a fake, serious tone, "On the count of three then, uno, dos, tres!"

And with that they both bit into the fiery treat. On fire now, they both grabbed for their water glasses and drained them.

Gina was there in a flash to refill them, "Gets me every time too, but it is good bite isn't it?"

Eyes still watering, they both nodded with smiles.

Leaving with full stomachs and better spirits they headed off to the Philadelphia Zoo. As an avid lover of all creatures great and small, Julia was excited for the opportunity to see some animals she had only read about up close. Miguel was excited for Julia, but not looking forward to the small mammal house where they had vampire bats. As a child his mother would tease him that the carnivorous bats would take him away if he didn't behave. He was not a fan of bats in the least bit. He secretly hoped they would miss that section of the zoo.

Since it was a school day, the zoo was not too crowded, just a few buses were parked in the lot after transporting kids on field trips.

Miguel got their tickets and the zoo map which was definitely not drawn to scale. Miguel pondered why they couldn't get such a simple thing right. He shook the thought away and came back to the present as he had much more important concerns. "Where should we go first mi pequeña," Miguel asked?

Julia pursed her lips as she studied the map, in moments like these Miguel could really see her mother.

"Well," she pondered, "if we turn left we can hit the Outback Outpost and then we can do the loop around the outer circle which has all the bigger animals. Then, we can do the inner circle and finish with the reptiles and amphibians.

Miguel shuddered; he knew what was in that last house, "Or maybe if we skip the reptiles and amphibians we'll have time to get your face painted," he said with hope.

She took the bribe, "Definitely, face painting Papa! The snakes are kind of icky anyway."

With that settled, they began their animal adventure. As they went through the exhibits Miguel could see how enamored she was with the animals. Julia asked the zookeepers many questions about what they ate and how they cared for their young. She was most enchanted with the flamingos, kangaroos and the giraffes. Miguel looked on with a smile but had a tight knot in his stomach. Forget about how bad it was going to be to tell Julia, how could he survive without her?

After she had a flamingo painted on her face, they sat on a bench to eat cream and watch the cloud animals. Miguel pointed to them and said, "Just think how many more animals we now have to play with."

Julia looked up at Miguel with concern, "Papa, why are you so sad in such a happy place?"

Miguel lowered his head, *"she knew, didn't she?"*

She put her little hand in his and said, "It is what it is Papa so please tell me."

Miguel drew a long slow breath, "Remember when I told you about the mistake I made not coming here with the right papers?" She nodded somberly so he continued, "Well, the judge decided that I can't stay here right now..." His voice faltered as he watched a tear start to roll down Julia's her face. He squeezed her hand, "I have to go back to Mexico." He trailed off again feeling sick, "Tomorrow." Miguel watched the pink flamingo slowly dissolve down the side of his daughter's cheek.

Julia freaked out. "Nooooo!" Julia frantically ran to get away from the words she never wanted to hear.

Miguel was crushed. This was not how he wanted his last moments with her to be. He chased after her, hoping not too many people noticed the outburst. *"All I need is another problem,"* he thought.

When he finally caught up to her, they sat for several minutes in with Julia sobbing in his arms. She was first to break the silence, "Can't I come with you," she whispered?

Miguel shook his head vigorously as his tears flowed freely now, "No conejita, remember I told you that it wouldn't be safe for you there. Bad people who don't like your papa might try to hurt you because they know it would hurt me."

She shook her head just as vigorously, "Then it isn't safe for you either!"

Miguel knew she was right, but he had make her feel better about his leaving. He felt guilty that one of his last conversations with his daughter would contain a lie, "The judge said it would be safe for an adult, just not children."

She started to protest, "But then I can come, I can be brave," she stomped a foot for emphasis.

Miguel ran his hand through her silky hair, "I need you to be brave for me here, until I can get back to you. It won't be forever, and we can video call each other every day. Can you be brave for me my sweet girl?"

Julia lay her head on Miguel's arm and with her a quivering voice she answered, "Si, Papa, sere valiente."

CHAPTER THIRTY-SEVEN

A few days later, Vinny called another meeting. "Well gang, it didn't take as long as we thought. I didn't want to say anything prematurely," Vinny paused to read the room. He liked to build a little anticipation for his findings.

"We are still working to crack the encryption used by The Collective. But fortunately, when they communicated with the *Our Truth News*, they weren't using encryption. Their communications were wide open!" Vinny said gleefully.

After Fox News started to wake up to President Trump's game and started rightfully criticizing him for his gross inaccuracies, blatant lies, and anti-conservative behavior, Trump soured on them. Reporters with integrity, like Shepard Smith, were now the enemy. Even the bootlicker Tucker Carlson reached his limit when Trump openly, and unapologetically asked for political help from the Ukraine and China stating, "There's no way to spin this."[xli]

Other news outlets emerged as his favorites and took over the mantle of sycophant behavior. Their outright praise of everything Trump made their station a permanent fixture in the White House.

Vinny continued, "Well, President Trump doesn't hide his love for *Our Truth News*, but apparently The Collective loves them as well."

Alex didn't see the connection. "Why would The Collective care about a news network? Especially one with such low regard for facts. Who takes them seriously?"

"Well for starters, they are more than comfortable with their distorting the record to push their pro-business agenda," explained Vinny.

"But is Trump's agenda really pro-business? He reversed years of strong Republican support for free trade. His tariff-based economy led to bailouts to farmers that have cost more than double what Obama's 'Socialist' bailout of the auto industry cost the US taxpayers. That wasn't good for businesses."[xlii]

"You're preaching to the choir Alex. President Trump is picking winners. He's chosen industries like coal to subsidize over cheaper and safer sources of energy like natural gas and renewable sources," replied Vinny.[xliii]

Traya chimed in, "God forbid Trump did anything that would be positive for the environment. We've all seen the studies, on the hypocrisy of right-wing states crying out against the left's purported agenda, while accepting far more in federal tax dollars than their liberal counterparts."[xliv]

"So how does The Collective fit in?" asked Caroline who had been silent until now.

Vinny was happy to explain, "The Collective is picking winners as well."

Vinny posted a few of the most damming texts from The Collective to various hosts. The first one focused on one of the right wing's favorite conspiracy theories that environmentalists push saving the environment not to preserve the world for future generations, but as a system to redistribute wealth from the rich to the poor. The theory even extends to the world being ruled by one government with sovereign nationals vanishing from the Earth.

```
RichardNunn to StoppedBelievingInScience:
```

```
Focus on: climate change is a hoax. Left wing
agenda to create a one-world government.
America can't afford a Green New Deal.
```

Traya could never resist commenting on the environment. "Well I think Trump didn't need much help with that one. His push to open protected lands falls right into The Collective's playbook. They could then rape the land for short term gain regardless of the scars left to once pristine lands."

"All highly probably Traya. I have one more email:"

```
SVK ->IHaveNoSoul:
```

```
Focus on: Tariffs are good for the economy.
They are paid for by the Chinese companies.
Huge windfall for Treasury.
```

"That's ridiculous," Tano declared. "I'm tired of Trump stating that the tariffs are being paid for by the Chinese manufacturers. That's not how tariffs work. The cost of the tariff is just added to the cost of the product and paid by the working class while the fat heads get fatter."

Tariffs were a hidden tax. So once again, Republicans claimed to lower taxes, but in reality are raising them on the poor. The last time this occurred was when Reagan lowered taxes on the rich, but raised the Social Security and Medicare taxes so much that the poor saw a tax increase from his cut.[xlv]

Given *Our Truth News'* constant praise of Trump, the president was easily swayed into taking stances they preached as if they were his ideas to begin with. This was similar, to some degree, with Trump's friendships and meetings with Fox personalities, but *Our Truth* took it to a new level.

Vinny explained, "It would seem that our friends at The Collective are curating what is covered on *Our Truth News*."

"Well given Trump's ease of being manipulated by a compliment, that narcissist policies are being influenced by The Collective as well," Alex said.

Trump was not the truly "stable genius" he purported everyone said he was. Funny, how there are no quotes from "everyone" calling him that. Maybe "everyone" were people like John Barron, John Miller, Carolin Gallego or David Dennison. They were all pseudonyms used by President Trump or his once lawyer Michael Cohen to promote himself.[xlvi] Instead he was closer to the *useful idiot* as he was dubbed by the left-wing media.

The Collective took advantage at every turn to capitalize on Trump's actions. From accelerating the value of their land purchases, to timing investments in stocks like gun companies days before public controversies arose, The Collective was always two, or three steps ahead.

"The problem is they haven't broken any laws," Alex cried out in frustration.

"Sadly, that's true. As Trump would say, 'No crime here,'" Vinny added.

"What was it that Maya Angelou said?" Traya asked.

"When someone shows you who they are believe them; the first time." Alex proclaimed. Indeed, Trump is who we first saw him as, he never grew into the presidency, never tried to grow his support, instead he stayed the thin-skinned, TV watching blowhard who doesn't read and prefers to follow his id over reasoning over facts.

"Yeah and it's the country and the world that gets Zojjed," denounced Alex.

"You still trying to make that word part of the vernacular?" asked Vinny.

"You know it!" answered Alex.

"Well maybe in today's meme world if you attached it to an image of President Trump it will get some legs," offered Vinny about the made up word Alex and her friends created in college to describe when they are completely screwed over.

CHAPTER THIRTY-EIGHT

Sitting on the tarmac, Miguel stared out the window of the plane as it waited endlessly for an open gate at Mexico City's Benito Juarez airport. Delays were common as they rarely had enough gates open for incoming planes. The incessant chatter of the young guy sitting next to him had stopped at least. While Miguel would normally welcome a friendly conversation, he was in no mood for small talk and certainly didn't want to discuss what he was going to do in Mexico with someone headed for an all-inclusive vacation.

Everyone around him was agitated, but Miguel was in no rush. He was content to sit peacefully in his seat before the reality of the rest of his life intruded.

When the plane finally pulled up to the gate and the chime to remove your safety belts triggered a rush of frenzied passengers to get their carry-on luggage, Miguel just stayed put. His dream of safely living in the USA was over, he was separated from his daughter, and he had no prospects for employment. At least his little Julia was safe with his aunt. Miguel looked out of the window and up at the clouds. He wondered if they would ever look at them together again.

As the plane emptied, he turned on his phone. He texted his mom that he was on his way out. Fortunately, his cell phone came with coverage of Mexico and Canada by default so at least for the time being he could communicate easily with not only his mother in Mexico, but with his aunt as well. *"How can I call Julia?"* he wondered to himself. *"Will she hate me for leaving her?"* These internal questions just repeated themselves in his head.

A dejected Miguel walked lethargically off the plane. He always dreamed of what his first flight would be like. This wasn't exactly the thrill he dreamed, but at least he would see his mother for the first time in over a decade.

He had no luggage, no belongings other than what he had on him. When he made it through customs, his mom was waiting. Tears, both of joy and sorrow, were running down her weathered face. The pictures he received over the years didn't do justice. She aged far more than he could tell from photographs.

He gave her a big hug. She clutched him even harder. *"Well she hasn't lost any of her strength,"* thought Miguel remembering the whooping he used to regularly get when he misbehaved.

Miguel's mom whispered, "Don't worry my love. God will provide. You will see, you will be ok." His mom was always the optimist, even in the worst of times.

Miguel didn't answer. *"How could he dash his mother's hopes? Would he be forced into a gang? Would they remember him?"*

 Just then then his phone vibrated. A text message came in from an unknown number.

```
Miguel. We understand you are recently back in
Mexico and are looking for employment. We have
a job offer for you that will take advantage of
you strong bilingual skills. If interested in a
comfortable job with reasonable pay, and a safe
place for you and your mom to live. Text back
YES and we'll set you up to start for DataRex
next week.
```

"How could that be?" Miguel questioned as he showed his mother the text.

"No se, Miguel, but I wouldn't turn it down. You see I told you God would provide," replied his mom.

"Which of my friends did you tell I was coming home? This would be just the kind of joke his friends would play." Most of Miguel's childhood friends never got out of Mexico and those that were still alive were living near his mother.

"I never told any of them you were coming back. I lost contact with most of them over the years," explained his mom.

Miguel texted back YES!

CHAPTER THIRTY-NINE

As the months progressed *Our Truth News'* reporting had no issues with Trump's flagrant disregard for family values. His alleged sexual misconduct, three marriages, and inappropriate language were all topics that went without mention in their coverage. When Trump blatantly asked other countries to investigate his political foes, they praised it as the only reasonable thing to do to drain the swamp.

Any in-depth search of their website finds it devoid of any embarrassing remarks President Trump said or tweeted. If Fox News' audience lived in a bubble, one could only imagine the microscopic view of the world of the average *Our Truth* viewer.

Homeland Security uncovered more messages from The Collective to *Our Truth News* to push their agenda.

```
RichardNunn to MyTieIsTooLong:

Focus on: The socialists want to take your
guns! All of them, not just the AK-47s.
```

If you want to endear yourself with the right, no message worked better than to quote a democrat threatening to take all guns away. When Beto O'Rourke said "Hell, yes, we're going to take your AR-15, your AK-47" it doomed many an effort for sensible gun regulations. The right used statements like O'Rourke's to fire up the base.

Vinny was able to at least tie one directive that The Collective sent to all the hosts to financial transactions as well.

```
RichardNunn to MyTieIsTooLong, IHaveNoSoul, &
StoppedBelievingInScience

Mention AOC and Omar as much as possible as the
face of the Democratic party.
```

Nothing riled up *Our Truth*'s audience more than mentioning any of the four young women Democratic representatives known as the 'Squad.' Their far left ideology and perhaps darker skin color made any right-wing nutjob enraged with a frantic disdain that most reserve for Satan incarnate. Some of their progressive ideas might be unrealistic in the timeframe they wish to accomplish them, but if Kennedy didn't reach for the moon, would we have ever gotten there?

While the right tries to brand the left as crazed socialists, the reality is the left is proposing big government programs, not real socialism. When Trump suggested that companies in the USA redirect their supply chain the network was quiet again. The true meaning of socialism is a system where the government has "ownership and administration of the means of production and distribution of goods." [xlvii] With this blatant attempt by President Trump to control how our economy operates, one might think the anti-socialists would be outraged.

The Collective took it even further. They were also behind funding AOC, Omar and the rest of the Squad. The grass roots effort was really a carefully orchestrated network of donors funneling campaign funds. Even the Squad had no idea the true source of their funding. There was nothing like putting a mouthpiece for the left front and center to fire up the radical right base and make the liberals look bad.

The Collective's funding of DataRex was nothing more than a clever plan to manipulate not just public opinion, but Trump's as well. What better cover for The Collective than to have the President unknowingly be a pawn in the bigger game. By creating an endless stream of anti-Democrat posts, memes and Tweets, The Collective didn't even need to intentionally push them Trump's way. With others thrusting them out to the masses, Trump had his canned response whenever someone challenged the veracity of his repost and sometimes he'd punt claiming the source was "a highly respected conservative pundit."[xlviii]

CHAPTER FORTY

Who but the most conspiracy-minded of people could have put the string of events together? Trump's hard stance against illegal, and in many cases legal immigration created an environment for cheap, educated labor across the border. Just as he capitalized on cheap labor for his Chinese manufactured goods, he created a desperate, educated workforce by forcing illegal immigrants that had matured their command of English after living in the USA for years back to Mexico where they had to accept whatever jobs were available. The racist overtones stoked a hidden sentiment buried just below the surface making it easy to gloss over the atrocities caused by such cruel-hearted policies. Illegal immigrants who lived in the USA were the perfect workforce for Trump's "fake news" campaign.

Given the repetitive outlandish claims Trump made on a daily basis, some estimates that are higher than a dozen false or misleading claims a day[xlix], it was impossible for people to keep track of one deflection from another. Once The Collective added their own agenda to the mix, who would notice?

When Trump proposed buying Greenland, asking a room of people, "Do you think it would work?" most in attendance assumed he was joking.[l] The Prime minister of Denmark Mette Frederiksen wasn't laughing when she called the idea "absurd." However, it was the tip of an iceberg of The Collective's sinister plan. While Trump was making news proposing buying Greenland, the public was distracted while The Collective was busy buying up mineral-rich or fertile lands soon to be easily accessible by climate change.

Trump's trade wars seemed unrelated, but served multiple purposes. By causing China to divert the purchase of soybeans from the USA to Brazil, the acceleration of the deforestation of the rain forest followed. Destroying the lungs of the world, accelerated global warming was wreaking havoc on traditional agricultural strongholds while surreptitiously opening new fertile lands. Not just in Greenland, but across many northern lands like Canada and, how conveniently, Russia. With numerous business entities under The Collective's umbrella buying up land on the cheap, it appears they didn't ignore the reports by NASA predicting global environmental disaster. Instead, they paid close attention and capitalized on it. Pushing bogus concepts like Clean Coal and a return to energies of yesteryear just accelerated the process even more. Of course, as per The Collective's suggestions, the *Our Truth* network continued to report that there was no global warming.

When Bill Gates was on the precipice of endless, safe energy generation with no greenhouse gas emissions, The Collective simply stoked the anti-China sentiment to convince President Trump to rescind the technology transfer allowing the prototype plant to be built in China.

Trump renegotiated NAFTA. Instead of highlighting the benefits to the USA, he focused on what it was called and how the agreement's name sounded. Given that Trump previously questioned anyone's sanity to have signed it, it was a hollow victory, but one that left the ability to replace a Chinese workforce with a Mexican one.

With the selective use of exceptions to tariffs Trump was once again pushing a socialist agenda by picking favorites and thus controlling the processes of manufacture and distribution in the USA. Trump cooled industries with rapid growth like solar, but conveniently exempted plastic straws from the tariff. Perhaps it was a stab at environmentalists who sought to ban their use.

Trump talked about the Fake News media and he blamed it on a 500 pound guy in China. Both were brilliant deflections from the man that not only invented fake news, but took it to levels beyond comprehension.

Without a smoking gun to catch The Collective, Vinny needed to bring someone down to justify that he got results from the investigation. The obvious fall guy was DataRex's Lechtenberg. If nothing else they could prosecute him under California's new laws against creating deep fakes.

CHAPTER FORTY-ONE

That summer Alex landed in Toronto to compete at the World Masters Championships. Turning 35 was a blessing and a curse. No woman likes to see the hands of time move forward, but as a race walker there was a completely new set of competitive doors open. In this case it was the Masters competitions for those 35 years of age and older.

Masters races were organized by age groups, providing more "mature" athletes the opportunity to compete on a more balanced playing field. When she was a younger athlete, Alex thought it was a giant money grab, but now faced with a body that couldn't keep up with many of the younger athletes she saw the value. *"Perhaps the Baby Boomers and Gen Xers learned something from the millennial mentality that everyone deserves a trophy for showing up,"* thought Alex.

In reality, it gave her a much greater reach to travel around the world under her alias.

Just then she met up with a group of race walkers she knew from previous races and online "friendships." There was a small contingent from the USA talking to a bunch of Canadians. Intermixed within the group were a few walkers from England, France and Eastern Europe.

Alex said hello to all and then wasted no time approaching Olek Anastas from the Ukraine. "Hey Olek, nice to finally meet ya. Want to do some gaming tonight?"

EPILOGUE

While one wouldn't normally write an explanation at the end of a novel, the methodology used to create this story warrants expounding. Wherever possible we tried to cite references to facts used in the story. Our goal was to use as many citations from FoxNews.com to remove the perceived liberal bias.

We are horrified to state that even finding simple facts, like exact quotes, that were demeaning to the Trump agenda were not accessible via their search engine.

A perfect example was when looking for the quote "There's no good way to spin this," which was said by Fox News host Tucker Carlson it was nowhere to be found. When we tried to search "Carlson Ukraine Trump China," plenty appeared about Joe Biden and his son golfing with a Ukrainian businessman as well as many other anti-Biden/Democratic slanted articles.

Perhaps their search technology is not up to snuff, but we suspect it is far more likely that the facts are just not there. The lack of coverage certainly isn't a lie, but it does help to explain why so many Trumpers support him and don't question his behavior. They are often unaware of it.

BIBLIOGRAPHY

[i] Linthicum, K. (2018, 05 24). *La Times*. Retrieved from La Times: https://www.latimes.com/world/la-fg-mexico-guns-20180524-story.html

[ii] Diaz, D. (2017, 5 25). *CNN*. Retrieved from CNN: https://www.cnn.com/2017/05/25/politics/trump-pushes-prime-minister-nato-summit/index.html

[iii] Shrikant, A. (2015, 9 8). *Why some people don't tip their Uber drivers*. Retrieved from Vox: https://www.vox.com/the-goods/2018/10/8/17952804/why-some-people-dont-tip-their-uber-drivers

[iv] *Liberty Headlines*. (2017, 12 13). Retrieved from Liberty Headlines: https://www.libertyheadlines.com/texts-show-fbi-officials-exchanged-insults-trump-last-year/

[v] Stimson, B. (2019, 3 19). *Fox News*. Retrieved from Fox News: https://www.foxnews.com/politics/ronald-reagans-daughter-says-father-would-be-heartbroken-by-trumps-presidency

[vi] *ridester.com*. (2019, 09 04). Retrieved from ridester.com: https://www.ridester.com/how-much-do-uber-drivers-make/

[vii] *Wikipedia*. (2019, 9 15). Retrieved from Wikipedia: https://en.wikipedia.org/wiki/Coyote_(person)

[viii] *Quartz*. (06, 10 2019). Retrieved from Quartz: https://qz.com/1632508/this-is-how-much-it-costs-to-cross-the-us-mexico-border-illegally/

[ix] *New York Times*. (2019, 06 26). Retrieved from New York Times: https://www.nytimes.com/2019/06/26/sports/trump-megan-rapinoe-tweet.html

[x] *NJ.com*. (2019, 06 26). Retrieved from NJ.com: https://www.nj.com/sports/2019/06/the-inevitable-donald-trump-

tweets-attacking-uswnts-womens-world-cup-star-megan-rapinoe-
have-arrived.html

xi *Wikipedia- TerraPower*. (2019, 10 02). Retrieved from Wikipedia:
https://en.wikipedia.org/wiki/TerraPower

xii Mazzaccaro, P. (2017, 06 14). *Chestnut Hill Local*. Retrieved from Chestnut
Hill Local: https://www.chestnuthilllocal.com/2017/06/14/party-
lines-drawn-on-suburban-lawns/

xiii Helmore, E. (2019, 9 13). *The Guardian*. Retrieved from The Guardian:
https://www.theguardian.com/us-news/2019/sep/13/trump-
orange-skin-hue-lightbulbs-energy-efficient

xiv Leibovich, M. (2019, 02 25). *New York Times*. Retrieved from New York
Times: https://www.nytimes.com/2019/02/25/magazine/lindsey-
graham-what-happened-trump.html

xv *Atlanta. News. Now*. (2016, 03 03). Retrieved from Atlanta. News. Now:
https://www.ajc.com/news/national/what-did-mitt-romney-say-
about-donald-trump/uxHPWFxhc2RFsBnuN6dNHI/

xvi *Mediaite*. (2019, 09 13). Retrieved from Mediaite:
https://www.mediaite.com/tv/lou-dobbs-tees-off-on-romney-
saying-he-wont-endorse-in-2020-what-is-wrong-with-this-man/

xvii Akeem, Z. (2019, 9 5). *Romney slammed Trump on Ukraine and China.
Now Trump wants Romney impeached*. Retrieved from Vox:
https://www.vox.com/2019/10/5/20900313/trump-romney-
ukraine-china-impeachment-tweets

xviii Makela, M. (2016, 10 08). *NY Times*. Retrieved from NY Times:
https://www.nytimes.com/2016/10/08/us/donald-trump-tape-
transcript.html

xix MEHTA, H. (2017, 08 25). *Friendly Atheist*. Retrieved from Friendly Atheist:
https://friendlyatheist.patheos.com/2017/08/25/christian-
textbook-urges-readers-to-keep-a-closed-
mind/?fbclid=IwAR3rxhdlO0ucPxXRLtMiGM8q_Evnl0YgfeytLScuJRF6
8GAA7mtc_-6nnq0

[xx] *Politico*. (2019, 08 26). Retrieved from Politico: https://www.politico.com/story/2019/08/26/white-house-melania-trump-kim-jong-un-1475726

[xxi] Sieff, K. (2019, 09 13). *The Washington Post*. Retrieved from The Washington Post: https://www.washingtonpost.com/world/the_americas/us-is-denying-passports-to-americans-along-the-border-throwing-their-citizenship-into-question/2018/08/29/1d630e84-a0da-11e8-a3dd-2a1991f075d5_story.html?noredirect=on

[xxii] Glass, J. (2014, 02 14). *8 Ways Porn Influenced Technology*. Retrieved from Trillist.com: https://www.thrillist.com/vice/how-porn-influenced-technology-8-ways-porn-influenced-tech-supercompressor-com

[xxiii] Institute, M. L. (2016, 05). *Mass Legal Help*. Retrieved from Mass Legal Help: https://www.masslegalhelp.org/immigration/notario

[xxiv] *CNN*. (2019, 09 03). Retrieved from CNN: https://www.cnn.com/2019/09/03/politics/donald-trump-golf-hurricane/index.html

[xxv] presidentialgolftracker. (2019, 09 04). *presidentialgolftracker*. Retrieved from presidentialgolftracker: https://presidentialgolftracker.com/trump-vs-obama-golf-games/

[xxvi] *Politico*. (2017, 02 21). Retrieved from Politico: https://www.politico.com/story/2017/02/trump-obama-golf-235217

[xxvii] *Cnet.com*. (2018, 12 17). Retrieved from Cnet: https://www.cnet.com/news/russian-influencers-thrived-on-instagram-after-pressure-on-facebook-twitter/

[xxviii] Stewart, E. (2019, 02 2019). *Vox*. Retrieved from Vox: https://www.vox.com/policy-and-politics/2019/1/30/18203611/trump-jobs-numbers-obama-economy-state-of-the-union

xxix Greszler, R. (2017, 12 21). *Heritage.org*. Retrieved from Heritage.org: https://www.heritage.org/budget-and-spending/commentary/how-big-your-states-share-6-trillion-unfunded-pension-liabilities

xxx Clarke, C. (2014, 02). *Is the Foreign Intelligence Surveillance Court Really a Rubber Stamp?* Retrieved from Standford Law Review: https://www.stanfordlawreview.org/online/is-the-foreign-intelligence-surveillance-court-really-a-rubber-stamp/

xxxi Nowrasteh, A. (2019, 03 04). *Cato Institute*. Retrieved from Cato Institute: https://www.cato.org/blog/illegal-immigrants-crime-assessing-evidence

xxxii *nolo.com*. (2019, 09 28). Retrieved from nolo.com: https://www.nolo.com/legal-encyclopedia/what-happens-bond-hearing-immigration-court.html

xxxiii *The Living Moon*. (2008). Retrieved from The Living Moon: https://www.thelivingmoon.com/41pegasus/02files/Global_Warming_003.html?fbclid=IwAR2a4_0pr6ECJ13bHOr65bWCzL7_pG9ZQoZc6Yi1ew-q8QDvxIbh4LDTPfM

xxxiv Press, A. (2012, 05 04). *Daily Mail*. Retrieved from Daily Mail: https://www.dailymail.co.uk/news/article-2139876/Mexico-drug-war-9-bodies-hanged-bridge-14-decapitated-heads-found.html

xxxv Kleyman, K. (2019, 10 03). *18 Terrifying Facts & Stories About MS-13, the World's Most Notorious Gang* . Retrieved from Ranker: https://www.ranker.com/list/mara-salvatrucha-facts-and-stories/katia-kleyman

xxxvi *Mexico 2017/2018*. (2019, 10 05). Retrieved from Amnesty International: https://www.amnesty.org/en/countries/americas/mexico/report-mexico/

xxxvii Linthicum, K. (2019, 03 14). *Five of the six most violent cities in the world are in Mexico, report says*. Retrieved from Los Angles Times: https://www.latimes.com/world/la-fg-mexico-tijuana-violence-20190314-story.html

xxxviii *Homicides surge in Mexico City: worst four-month period in 20 years.* (2018, 05 31). Retrieved from Mexico News Daily: https://mexiconewsdaily.com/news/violence-surges-in-mexico-city-worst-in-20-years/

xxxix *The Intercept.* (2016, 08 03). Retrieved from The Intercept: https://theintercept.com/2016/08/03/citizens-united-foreign-money-us-elections/

xxxx Hawkins, D. (2017, 04 25). *Washington Post.* Retrieved from Chobani sues Alex Jones, saying he falsely linked company to child rape, tuberculosis: https://www.washingtonpost.com/news/morning-mix/wp/2017/04/25/chobani-sues-alex-jones-saying-he-falsely-linked-company-to-child-rape-tuberculosis/

xxxxi Darcy, O. (2019, 10 5). *CNN.* Retrieved from CNN: https://www.cnn.com/2019/10/05/media/tucker-carlson-op-ed-ukraine-trump-impeachment/index.html

xxxxii *The Week.* (2019, 09 20). Retrieved from The Wek: https://theweek.com/speedreads/866567/trumps-farmer-bailout-already-more-than-twice-expensive-obamas-automaker-bailout

xxxxiii Marcacci, S. (2017, 11 06). *Forbes.* Retrieved from Forbes: https://www.forbes.com/sites/energyinnovation/2017/11/06/rick-perrys-coal-and-nuclear-subsidy-could-cost-10-billion-per-year-is-america-great-again-yet/#6f5a2dd230db

xxxxiv Ohlemacher, S. (2017, 12 09). *AP.* Retrieved from AP: https://www.apnews.com/2f83c72de1bd440d92cdbc0d3b6bc08c

xxxxv *SSA.* (2019, 09 20). Retrieved from SSA: https://www.ssa.gov/history/1983amend.html

xxxxvi *Wikipedia.* (2019, 10 4). Retrieved from Wikipedia: https://en.wikipedia.org/wiki/Pseudonyms_of_Donald_Trump

xxxxvii *Merriam-Webster.* (2019, 20 9). Retrieved from Merriam-Webster: https://www.merriam-webster.com/dictionary/socialism

xxxxviii Blumberg, A. (2019, 8 13). *Huffington Post*. Retrieved from Huffington Post: https://www.huffpost.com/entry/trump-defends-epstein-retweet-clinton-conspiracy_n_5d52e3d1e4b05fa9df056ccb

xxxxix *Washington Post*. (2019, 08 12). Retrieved from Washington Post: https://www.washingtonpost.com/politics/2019/08/12/president-trump-has-made-false-or-misleading-claims-over-days/?noredirect=on

l *NBC News*. (2019, 8 15). Retrieved from NBC News: https://www.nbcnews.com/politics/donald-trump/trump-s-green-new-deal-president-reportedly-considering-buying-greenland-n1042966

ADDITIONAL PUBLICATIONS BY SALVAGE AMERICA PUBLICATIONS

"We save democracy one page at a time!"

The *Parable of the Peacock* takes a satirical look at the state of American politics as we approach the critical 2020 presidential election. Written in the style of a children's picture book, the work's rhyming couplets are best enjoyed read aloud. The book serves up ridicule to deserving parties, but it saves a heaping plateful for the *Mocker-in-Chief*.

THE PARABLE OF THE PEACOCK

A Read-Aloud Picture Book for 2020 Voters

Written by Brent Bohlen
Illustrated by Oksana Basarab

For more information visit www.peacockparable.com.

The Parable of the Peacock is a 36 page, 8" x 10" full-color paperback book.

You can order it from www.amazon.com or your local bookstore.

[i] Linthicum, K. (2018, 05 24). *La Times*. Retrieved from La Times: https://www.latimes.com/world/la-fg-mexico-guns-20180524-story.html

[ii] Diaz, D. (2017, 5 25). *CNN*. Retrieved from CNN: https://www.cnn.com/2017/05/25/politics/trump-pushes-prime-minister-nato-summit/index.html

[iii] Shrikant, A. (2015, 9 8). *Why some people don't tip their Uber drivers*. Retrieved from Vox: https://www.vox.com/the-goods/2018/10/8/17952804/why-some-people-dont-tip-their-uber-drivers

[iv] *Liberty Headlines*. (2017, 12 13). Retrieved from Liberty Headlines: https://www.libertyheadlines.com/texts-show-fbi-officials-exchanged-insults-trump-last-year/

[v] Stimson, B. (2019, 3 19). *Fox News*. Retrieved from Fox News: https://www.foxnews.com/politics/ronald-reagans-daughter-says-father-would-be-heartbroken-by-trumps-presidency

[vi] *ridester.com*. (2019, 09 04). Retrieved from ridester.com: https://www.ridester.com/how-much-do-uber-drivers-make/

[vii] *Wikipedia*. (2019, 9 15). Retrieved from Wikipedia: https://en.wikipedia.org/wiki/Coyote_(person)

[viii] *Quartz*. (06, 10 2019). Retrieved from Quartz: https://qz.com/1632508/this-is-how-much-it-costs-to-cross-the-us-mexico-border-illegally/

[ix] *New York Times*. (2019, 06 26). Retrieved from New York Times: https://www.nytimes.com/2019/06/26/sports/trump-megan-rapinoe-tweet.html

[x] *NJ.com*. (2019, 06 26). Retrieved from NJ.com: https://www.nj.com/sports/2019/06/the-inevitable-donald-trump-tweets-attacking-uswnts-womens-world-cup-star-megan-rapinoe-have-arrived.html

xi *Wikipedia- TerraPower*. (2019, 10 02). Retrieved from Wikipedia: https://en.wikipedia.org/wiki/TerraPower

xii Mazzaccaro, P. (2017, 06 14). *Chestnut Hill Local*. Retrieved from Chestnut Hill Local: https://www.chestnuthilllocal.com/2017/06/14/party-lines-drawn-on-suburban-lawns/

xiii Helmore, E. (2019, 9 13). *The Guardian*. Retrieved from The Guardian: https://www.theguardian.com/us-news/2019/sep/13/trump-orange-skin-hue-lightbulbs-energy-efficient

xiv Leibovich, M. (2019, 02 25). *New York Times*. Retrieved from New York Times: https://www.nytimes.com/2019/02/25/magazine/lindsey-graham-what-happened-trump.html

xv *Atlanta. News. Now*. (2016, 03 03). Retrieved from Atlanta. News. Now: https://www.ajc.com/news/national/what-did-mitt-romney-say-about-donald-trump/uxHPWFxhc2RFsBnuN6dNHI/

xvi *Mediaite*. (2019, 09 13). Retrieved from Mediaite: https://www.mediaite.com/tv/lou-dobbs-tees-off-on-romney-saying-he-wont-endorse-in-2020-what-is-wrong-with-this-man/

xvii Akeem, Z. (2019, 9 5). *Romney slammed Trump on Ukraine and China. Now Trump wants Romney impeached.* Retrieved from Vox: https://www.vox.com/2019/10/5/20900313/trump-romney-ukraine-china-impeachment-tweets

xviii Makela, M. (2016, 10 08). *NY Times*. Retrieved from NY Times: https://www.nytimes.com/2016/10/08/us/donald-trump-tape-transcript.html

xix MEHTA, H. (2017, 08 25). *Friendly Atheist*. Retrieved from Friendly Atheist: https://friendlyatheist.patheos.com/2017/08/25/christian-textbook-urges-readers-to-keep-a-closed-mind/?fbclid=IwAR3rxhdIO0ucPxXRLtMiGM8q_EvnI0YgfeytLScuJRF68GAA7mtc_-6nnq0 xx *Politico*. (2019, 08 26). Retrieved from Politico: https://www.politico.com/story/2019/08/26/white-house-melania-trump-kim-jong-un-1475726

xxi Sieff, K. (2019, 09 13). *The Washington Post*. Retrieved from The Washington Post: https://www.washingtonpost.com/world/the_americas/us-is-denying-passports-to-americans-along-the-border-throwing-their-citizenship-into-question/2018/08/29/1d630e84-a0da-11e8-a3dd-2a1991f075d5_story.html?noredirect=on

xxii Glass, J. (2014, 02 14). *8 Ways Porn Influenced Technology*. Retrieved from Trillist.com: https://www.thrillist.com/vice/how-porn-influenced-technology-8-ways-porn-influenced-tech-supercompressor-com

xxiii Institute, M. L. (2016, 05). *Mass Legal Help*. Retrieved from Mass Legal Help: https://www.masslegalhelp.org/immigration/notario

xxiv *CNN*. (2019, 09 03). Retrieved from CNN: https://www.cnn.com/2019/09/03/politics/donald-trump-golf-hurricane/index.html

xxv presidentialgolftracker. (2019, 09 04). *presidentialgolftracker*. Retrieved from presidentialgolftracker: https://presidentialgolftracker.com/trump-vs-obama-golf-games/

xxvi *Politico*. (2017, 02 21). Retrieved from Politico: https://www.politico.com/story/2017/02/trump-obama-golf-235217

xxvii *Cnet.com*. (2018, 12 17). Retrieved from Cnet: https://www.cnet.com/news/russian-influencers-thrived-on-instagram-after-pressure-on-facebook-twitter/

xxviii Stewart, E. (2019, 02 2019). *Vox*. Retrieved from Vox: https://www.vox.com/policy-and-politics/2019/1/30/18203611/trump-jobs-numbers-obama-economy-state-of-the-union xxix Greszler, R. (2017, 12 21). *Heritage.org*. Retrieved from Heritage.org: https://www.heritage.org/budget-and-spending/commentary/how-big-your-states-share-6-trillion-unfunded-pension-liabilities

xxx Clarke, C. (2014, 02). *Is the Foreign Intelligence Surveillance Court Really a Rubber Stamp?* Retrieved from Standford Law Review: https://www.stanfordlawreview.org/online/is-the-foreign-intelligence-surveillance-court-really-a-rubber-stamp/

xxxi Nowrasteh, A. (2019, 03 04). *Cato Institute*. Retrieved from Cato Institute: https://www.cato.org/blog/illegal-immigrants-crime-assessing-evidence

xxxii *nolo.com*. (2019, 09 28). Retrieved from nolo.com: https://www.nolo.com/legal-encyclopedia/what-happens-bond-hearing-immigration-court.html

xxxiii *The Living Moon*. (2008). Retrieved from The Living Moon: https://www.thelivingmoon.com/41pegasus/02files/Global_Warming_003.html?fbclid=IwAR2a4_0pr6ECJ13bHOr65bWCzL7_pG9ZQoZc6Yi1ew-q8QDvxIbh4LDTPfM

xxxiv Press, A. (2012, 05 04). *Daily Mail*. Retrieved from Daily Mail: https://www.dailymail.co.uk/news/article-2139876/Mexico-drug-war-9-bodies-hanged-bridge-14-decapitated-heads-found.html

xxxv Kleyman, K. (2019, 10 03). *18 Terrifying Facts & Stories About MS-13, the World's Most Notorious Gang* . Retrieved from Ranker: https://www.ranker.com/list/mara-salvatrucha-facts-and-stories/katia-kleyman

xxxvi *Mexico 2017/2018*. (2019, 10 05). Retrieved from Amnesty International: https://www.amnesty.org/en/countries/americas/mexico/report-mexico/

xxxvii Linthicum, K. (2019, 03 14). *Five of the six most violent cities in the world are in Mexico, report says*. Retrieved from Los Angles Times: https://www.latimes.com/world/la-fg-mexico-tijuana-violence-20190314-story.html

xxxviii *Homicides surge in Mexico City: worst four-month period in 20 years.* (2018, 05 31). Retrieved from Mexico News Daily: https://mexiconewsdaily.com/news/violence-surges-in-mexico-city-worst-in-20-years/

xxxix *The Intercept.* (2016, 08 03). Retrieved from The Intercept: https://theintercept.com/2016/08/03/citizens-united-foreign-money-us-elections/

xl Hawkins, D. (2017, 04 25). *Washington Post.* Retrieved from Chobani sues Alex Jones, saying he falsely linked company to child rape, tuberculosis: https://www.washingtonpost.com/news/morning-mix/wp/2017/04/25/chobani-sues-alex-jones-saying-he-falsely-linked-company-to-child-rape-tuberculosis/

xli Darcy, O. (2019, 10 5). *CNN.* Retrieved from CNN: https://www.cnn.com/2019/10/05/media/tucker-carlson-op-ed-ukraine-trump-impeachment/index.html

xlii *The Week.* (2019, 09 20). Retrieved from The Wek: https://theweek.com/speedreads/866567/trumps-farmer-bailout-already-more-than-twice-expensive-obamas-automaker-bailout

xliii Marcacci, S. (2017, 11 06). *Forbes.* Retrieved from Forbes: https://www.forbes.com/sites/energyinnovation/2017/11/06/rick-perrys-coal-and-nuclear-subsidy-could-cost-10-billion-per-year-is-america-great-again-yet/#6f5a2dd230db

xliv Ohlemacher, S. (2017, 12 09). *AP.* Retrieved from AP: https://www.apnews.com/2f83c72de1bd440d92cdbc0d3b6bc08c

xlv *SSA.* (2019, 09 20). Retrieved from SSA: https://www.ssa.gov/history/1983amend.html

xlvi *Wikipedia.* (2019, 10 4). Retrieved from Wikipedia: https://en.wikipedia.org/wiki/Pseudonyms_of_Donald_Trump

xlvii *Merriam-Webster.* (2019, 20 9). Retrieved from Merriam-Webster: https://www.merriam-webster.com/dictionary/socialism

xlviii Blumberg, A. (2019, 8 13). *Huffington Post*. Retrieved from Huffington Post: https://www.huffpost.com/entry/trump-defends-epstein-retweet-clinton-conspiracy_n_5d52e3d1e4b05fa9df056ccb

xlix *Washington Post*. (2019, 08 12). Retrieved from Washington Post: https://www.washingtonpost.com/politics/2019/08/12/president-trump-has-made-false-or-misleading-claims-over-days/?noredirect=on

l *NBC News*. (2019, 8 15). Retrieved from NBC News: https://www.nbcnews.com/politics/donald-trump/trump-s-green-new-deal-president-reportedly-considering-buying-greenland-n1042966

www.ingramcontent.com/pod-product-compliance
Lightning Source LLC
Chambersburg PA
CBHW061135200626
46817CB00016B/1647